T0400569

Julia's Joy

**Center Point
Large Print**

Also by Susan G Mathis and available from Center Point Large Print:

Libby's Lighthouse

Julia's Joy

LOVE AT A LIGHTHOUSE
BOOK TWO

SUSAN G MATHIS

CENTER POINT LARGE PRINT
THORNDIKE, MAINE

This Center Point Large Print edition
is published in the year 2025 by arrangement with
Wild Heart Books.

The text of this Large Print edition is unabridged.
In other aspects, this book may vary
from the original edition.
Printed in the United States of America
on permanent paper sourced using
environmentally responsible foresting methods.
Set in 16-point Times New Roman type.

ISBN: 979-8-89164-473-1

The Library of Congress has cataloged this record
under Library of Congress Control Number: 2024949803

Dedication

To my daughter, Janelle, who inspires me every day. When she was young, she loved lighthouses, and when her girls were little, we toured an iconic South African lighthouse with two dozen preschoolers, climbing the circular staircase in princess gowns and enjoying a snack inside. The day, the wonder of it, inspired me, and ever since then, I wanted to create lighthouse stories. Thanks, Janelle, for the memories.

To the Thousand Islands River Rats and my faithful readers who love the river as much as I do. Thanks for your support in reading my stories, sharing them with others, and writing reviews. You bless me.

Chapter 1

As the boat cut through the choppy waves, Julia Collins couldn't help but resent the place that would imprison her for the entire summer, thanks to Granny's wishes and the will that held her future in the balance. The elusive prize of a hefty inheritance dangled around her neck like a heavy golden chain, demanding her sacrifice.

She shifted in her seat to see little but water and an island in the distance. Her discontent matched the chilly, churning water around her as the boat sailed closer to Sister Island Lighthouse. Strung together like pearls on a bracelet, its three tiny islets were miles from her Canadian mainland home, and more than a mile from the New York shore, smack dab in the middle of nowhere in the mighty St. Lawrence River.

Perched on the eastern edge of the island, the lighthouse cottage appeared rather quaint from a distance. Its stone façade and steeply pitched roof hinted at a simpler life, one far removed from the lively city parties, the bustling shopping area, and the vibrant gaggle of people she thrived on. The charm of the cottage, however, only intensified her sense of imprisonment. Even the lighthouse tower, poking out of the center of the house, mocked her arrival.

What was she going to do there all summer? She'd been looking forward to lively romps about town with her friends, but now . . . this?

Why, Granny? Why?

As the boat docked, Julia reluctantly stepped onto the island, her distain echoing in the hollow clack of her shoes on the wooden planks.

She pressed a few coins into the boatman's hand as he unloaded her luggage, including her easel and art supplies. "Thank you, sir, for the ride. Have a safe journey home."

The stocky old sailor tipped his cap. "You're welcome, miss. Good day."

Julia sucked in a steadying breath. This barren piece of the world would be her new home for months?

Her new home held little to commend it. Concrete-and-rock break walls and cement walkways connected the three islets. And there were no other buildings besides the cottage and an old boathouse and shed. That was all . . . for miles and miles. It was as if the island itself conspired to keep her within its narrow boundaries, far from the exciting life she'd known and still craved.

Her heart raced as it had when a swarm of wasps had chased her last summer. Her skin prickled, but she steeled herself to endure the days ahead.

Mrs. Dodge, her granny's friend whom she

hadn't seen since the funeral, awaited her at the edge of the lawn waving her welcome. A dozen steps beyond her stood a man around Julia's age—her son, whom Julia had met briefly at the funeral. The older woman's eyes shone with a mixture of pity and sympathy, and her smile faltered, making Julia's stomach churn.

Ahead of her lay a summer sentence of solitude—but she couldn't deny that part of this banishment was her own fault, a consequence of her own foolish actions.

Mrs. Dodge cleared her throat, tugging her from her troubles. "Welcome to Sister Island Lighthouse. Come. I have soup on the stove and tea to chase the chill of travel away."

Julia nodded, picking up her valise of her most precious possessions, her art supplies and easel. She steeled herself to face the long, looming days ahead. She could do this. She had no choice but to do this—and endure until the end.

Julia pasted on a smile and squared her shoulders. "Thank you, Mrs. Dodge. I'm Julia Collins, Maybelle Collins's granddaughter."

Mrs. Dodge swiftly took Julia's easel. "I remember, dearie, and I'm sorry for your loss. But I'm happy to see we will have an artist in residence." Before Julia could respond, Mrs. Dodge turned to her son. "William, make your way down here and help with these bags, please. You're not a statue, my boy."

In a flash, the man leaped into motion. Swift as a gazelle, he joined his mother and herself, grabbing hold of Julia's bulkier bags. But before heading toward the cottage, he paused and fixed his assessment of her. What thoughts were running through his mind? She couldn't discern, so she took a moment to size him up as well.

Mrs. Dodge's son, the lightkeeper, possessed a striking physical presence, and his tall, sturdy frame hinted at strength and dignity. His eyes were a soothing shade of blue, the color of the river on a calm day, his strong brow and thin lips adding an intriguing contrast. His thick, coffee-brown hair curled around his ears, framing his face, and long, dark lashes accentuated the reflection of the river in his undiscernible stare.

Despite his handsome features, a scowl adorned his expression, giving an air of mystery and uncertainty to his demeanor. With a subtle shake of his head, the lightkeeper exuded an inhospitable aura, as if safeguarding a hidden secret amid the desolation of the island.

Mrs. Dodge playfully shook a finger at her son. "Hold on a second, young man. Where are your manners? Extend a cordial greeting to our guest, and a smile wouldn't hurt either. After all, she'll be a part of our family for the entire summer."

He seemed to be suppressing a huff. "I'm Light-keeper Dodge. Welcome." His voice remained monotone and guarded. He didn't smile.

Mrs. Dodge clicked her tongue. "Call him William. Everyone else does."

Julia masked a grin and curtsied. Mrs. Dodge might be petite, but she certainly was spirited. "Thank you, Mrs. Dodge. William."

Once mother and son nodded their acknowledgement, Julia followed Mrs. Dodge to the cottage with William bringing up the rear. As she did, the majestic presence of the lighthouse on Sister Island arrested her attention. The gray limestone structure stood proudly against the backdrop of the river landscape. The two-story dwelling and attached light tower created a harmonious union, blending seamlessly with the natural surroundings.

Stepping nearer, Julia marveled at the meticulous craftsmanship evident in every detail. Her architect father would have appreciated such skillful artistry, may he rest in peace. Proudly recalling the architectural designs her father often shared with her, Julia grinned. The intricate knowledge he'd taught her flooded her mind, and a spark of inspiration ignited within.

The foundation, composed of limestone blocks, merged with the rugged rock outcropping, grounding the entire structure. Beautifully dressed limestone adorned the building, giving it an air of timeless elegance. Julia marveled at the decorative trusses and brackets adorning each end of the gabled roof, hinting at elements of stick-style architecture. Heavy limestone lintels and sills framed the lighthouse's many windows, adding to its sturdiness and charm. Her father's love of architecture served her well.

She admired the tower rising from the northern center of the roof, creating a captivating silhouette. The corbeled stonework beneath the additional story of the ten-sided lantern room added a touch of sophistication to the structure. As she rounded the east side of the house, she glimpsed two inset gable dormers in the steeply pitched southern roof.

Perhaps she could capture the essence of this place on canvas. Maybe, just maybe, with each stroke of her paintbrush, she could transform this banishment into something beautiful. Maybe then, this desolate place wouldn't be so bad.

She shifted from one foot to another, considering from what angle she might sketch the house. Perhaps, with the long days ahead, she'd paint several versions of it.

The cottage exuded a sense of history and purpose, as if the lighthouse itself held the tales of countless journeys along the river. Julia lingered for another moment, taking in the details of the guardian of the river and the symbol of resilience against the elements.

Mrs. Dodge pulled her from her musings. "Are you coming, dear?"

Startled, Julia hurried to join her on the steps

of the porch that led to the one-story addition on the eastern side of the cottage. "I'm sorry. I was admiring your lighthouse. It is beautiful, Mrs. Dodge."

The woman chuckled as she held open a screen door. "It is, rather. And since you'll be a part of the family, you can call me Aunt Dee. It's less formal. Come into the kitchen and sit a spell."

Julia followed her into the sunny kitchen and set her valise on the counter. "Thank you. May I use your privy, please?"

Aunt Dee nodded, pointing toward the door. "Of course. It's outside, in the shed next to the boathouse."

Julia thanked her, and she stepped back outside. The wooden shed, a modest abode for a bathroom, bore the marks of time and weather, the paint having faded into subtle hues.

Goodness! An outside privy would be quite a change from her grandmother's fine indoor plumbing. Another aspect of her banishment.

Julia approached the entrance, her footsteps accompanied by the soft crunch of gravel. As she opened the door, a mixture of mustiness and the scent of aged wood accosted her. The interior revealed a functional yet compact space. A small window allowed slivers of natural light to filter in, diffusing to illuminate the vintage fixtures and turquoise patina of well-worn surfaces within. Against one wall, a shelf held neatly arranged supplies—buckets, cleaning tools, an old Sears catalogue and newspapers, an oil lamp, and other essentials.

When she returned to the cottage, a bowl of steaming vegetable soup and fresh bread awaited her. Aunt Dee motioned for her to sit. "After we eat, I'll show you your room and the rest of the cottage. This place may not be what you're used to, but I hope it'll do for a summer on the island."

It would have to do if she was to get her inheritance. "Thank you for having me. My grandmother spoke so highly of you and the beauty of the river."

William tore a few pieces off the heel of bread and plopped it into his soup. "Your grandmother was correct. It's wonderful here."

The meal continued with stilted small talk that refused to settle her. Aunt Dee chattered about small things that mattered little to Julia. William barely said a word, eying her undiscernibly. She couldn't imagine an entire summer of this, and she already missed the city gossip. Would every meal be this awkward? If so, she'd suffer from indigestion daily.

When they were done, Aunt Dee stood and set her bowl in the sink. "William, please clear the table while I show Julia her room."

He nodded, picking up his dish. "Happy to. Thanks for lunch." He caught Julia's eye, a half smile gracing his lips.

Perhaps he'd thaw sooner rather than later? She hoped so.

Julia picked up her valise of art supplies and followed Aunt Dee up the narrow staircase to a tiny hallway. Three doors and another staircase fed off of it. Aunt Dee motioned toward each room. "This is my room, William's room, and your room. The stairs lead to the lighthouse tower." She opened the second door on the right. "I hope you like it. The dormer gives you a lovely view of the main channel and New York beyond."

The small room held only a single bed, dresser, and small desk with a chair. But Aunt Dee was correct. The view was spectacular. "It's lovely. Thanks again for hosting me."

Aunt Dee waved a dismissive hand. "Stuff and nonsense. No hosting to it. You're family now. Get settled and have a rest. I'll be downstairs if you need anything."

Julia set her case on the desk and plunked down on the bed, heaving a weary sigh. It was beautiful out here, to be sure, but the isolation closed in on her. Indeed, this place was more prison than paradise. Would obtaining her Granny's inheritance prove too costly to spend a summer in such simplicity, solitude, and starkness?

William lowered the kitchen window against the rain before taking a seat across from Julia and his mother at the worn wooden dinner table. Mother

15

passed the mashed potatoes, and he spooned a heaping mound onto his plate. Then he poured rich brown gravy liberally over it.

Julia placed a child's portion onto her plate next to a tiny piece of fish. No wonder she was so petite. She ladled a spoonful of canned beans onto her plate and stabbed a few with her fork. Her melancholy permeated the kitchen, but he held back his annoyance of it.

Her beauty, however, was another matter, one he'd ruminated over all afternoon. One that had captured his dreams ever since he'd met her at her grandmother's funeral. Despite her mood, Julia illuminated a room like the lighthouse beam itself.

Julia glanced around the unfamiliar surroundings before taking a bite, a slight furrow in her brow. She pasted on a forced smile. "This is good, Aunt Dee. Thank you." Her tone was flat. Her countenance flatter. What was so bad about being on the island?

He speared a forkful of grilled fish as Julia tentatively poked at her own plate, clearly unaccustomed to such simple fare. "I caught them just this morning. There's nothing like fresh fish."

Julia patted her lips daintily with her napkin. Her proper city manners seemed out of place in this casual island setting, and a touch of amusement mixed with a pang of empathy. The girl was definitely out of her element.

William cleared his throat and attempted to break the awkward silence that had settled between them. "What do you think of Sister Island?"

Julia's gaze flicked up, her lips quirking into a faltering smile. "It certainly is pretty." Her voice quivered. "Grandmother insisted I needed a change of scenery. A break from the hustle and bustle of the city. That's certainly true here."

He nodded, pretending to understand. What would drive a city girl like her to agree to come to a quiet place like this?

He listened as Julia and Mother conversed about Julia's grandmother, hoping to find a clue. Clearly, she loved her grandmother, and despite her obvious discomfort with being here, she spoke with determination to abide by her grandmother's wishes that she had penned in her will. Moreover, a quiet resilience seemed to infuse her. There was something undeniably intriguing about this woman.

But as she talked, her eyes and hair captivated him most. Like Mother's gingersnaps, her big round eyes held an intensity and depth that hinted at the stories and emotions within her, and her Irish roots were evident in the sprinkling of freckles that adorned her delicate skin, creating a starry map that added to her charm. A foot shorter than his own six-foot-two, with a delicate frame, she was gracefully slender.

And her tresses—a thick waterfall of ginger

strands sparkling with a reddish tint, catching the early-evening light in a way that seemed almost magical. He could almost feel the softness of it under his fingertips, imagining it slipping through his hands.

"William, pass the beans, please." Mother yanked him from his musings.

He swallowed back his flusterment and handed her the bowl. "If you'll excuse me. With this rain, it's getting dark enough to light the lamp. Thank you for dinner, Mother. Julia, have a good evening."

Julia bobbed her head, licking her lips. "You, too, William. Good night." She promptly put her head down, avoiding his scrutiny.

He kissed his mother's cheek, left the room, and climbed the ladder to the lamp room. The soft rain pattered against the windowpanes as he lit the lamp, the gentle cadence adding to the quiet night in the tall tower. Up here, alone, he had time to think, to pray, to ponder. Three of his favorite pastimes.

An hour later, his mother joined him, handing him a cup of tea. "Thank you, Mother. It's just what I needed." He kissed her cheek, pleased to have her company.

For several minutes, William stood silently beside her, staring into the darkness beyond, the steam from his tea mingling with the cool air. He sipped the soothing drink, waiting for Mother to break the silence and share the concerns he sensed in her. Her countenance spoke of worry and apprehension. Whenever she looked like that, there was a story waiting to unfold.

"William, there's something I want to remind you about Julia." Mother's voice carried the burden of years gone by. "I want you to remember that she's been through more than her fair share of trials in her twenty-two years, so I urge you to have patience with her."

At the disquiet etching lines across her face, William frowned. "I know she lost her parents and grandmother."

His mother took a deep breath. "Julia lost her mother and father at the same time when she was only fourteen. A terrible accident claimed their lives, leaving her alone in this world. Can you imagine how tragic that must have been?"

He groaned with empathy and set his tea aside, giving his mother his full attention. "I forgot she was so young. I knew she lived with her granny and lost her a few months ago, but losing both her parents must have been an unimaginable tragedy for someone so young."

His mother's frown was tainted with sorrow. "Indeed, it was. Julia had to face the harsh reality of death far too soon. She became an orphan in one horrible moment, left to navigate the complexities of adolescence without the guiding hands of her parents. My friend, her granny, took her on, but the sickly woman hadn't been well for some years, so I imagine Julia had little direction growing up. And now, with her grandma gone, too, Julia has no one."

Silence lingered in the room, the reality of Julia's past settling between them like a heavy fog. Finally, Mother sighed. "It must have taken tremendous strength for Julia to overcome such a profound loss then, and now, to lose her grandmother too."

William's compassion surged. "I can't even fathom what she's going through, but I'm pleased her grandmother suggested she take a respite here for a while. I hope we can be a blessing to her."

Mother nodded, but a skeptical scowl flashed over her features. "I hope so. It may take time and patience for her to feel comfortable here. And William, her grandmother didn't just *suggest* she come here. It is a requirement for Julia to receive her inheritance."

He choked back his surprise. "Goodness. No wonder she's so melancholy."

Mother paused for a moment before continuing. "Though I don't know Julia well, I sense that she must be a remarkable young woman. But, William, please remember she carries deep scars of her past and is eight years younger than you are, so it's important that you approach her with proper judiciousness and understanding."

As the rain slowed to a sprinkle outside,

William saw Julia in a new light. Though he had resolved to keep a cautious emotional distance, now he determined to be kind and supportive during her stay.

Still, that might not be so easy. After the betrayal he had experienced with his former fiancée, Louise, how could he protect himself from such an intriguing woman? Louise had left a deep, painful mark, so he had to guard his heart. He had learned the hard way that love wasn't always reciprocated—especially when Louise jilted him for his physical challenges and soon married his best friend. After that, he had vowed to steer clear of any possible romantic entanglements, no matter what.

Yes, he would focus on offering friendship and support to Julia. But he would also carefully navigate the delicate balance between connection with her and his need for self-preservation.

He gave his mother a determined smile. "Thank you for sharing that with me. I'll do everything I can to be a friend to her."

Mother nodded, a blend of gratitude and hope in her features. "I believe you will, William. And I think Julia is blessed to have us in her life for this pivotal summer. Now, I'll take my leave. Good night, son."

Once his mother left, the soft hum of the lighthouse machinery reverberated in the tower as he stood alone, surveying the river below. The steady sweep of the beam across the water was a constant companion to his thoughts, providing comfort in the night.

As he continued to study the river below, he found himself smiling at thoughts of Julia. He was fascinated with how she moved with a certain grace, as if she glided through life with an elegance uniquely her own. And she was an artist? Oh, how he longed to see her at work, to watch her create a masterpiece on his island.

There was much to learn about her—of that, he was sure.

Lost in his contemplation, William's heart swelled with curiosity. In that quiet moment, with the river stretching out before him, he silently vowed that, while keeping her at a safe distance, he would be a steady light in her life, just as the lighthouse was for the ships navigating the waters below.

The hatch to the lighthouse tower creaked open, and Julia's head appeared against the soft shine of the lantern room, a genial smile greeting him as he put out his hand and helped her climb the ladder and step inside.

The light emanating from the huge lamp caught her attention. "Goodness! I didn't realize how bright it is up here. It's dazzling."

"The fixed white light has a sixth-order Fresnel lens, so it projects a brilliant beam."

"And warmth." She swiped her brow with her

shirtsleeve, and her voice, soft in the quiet space, sounded almost like a little girl's. "I thought I'd check in before retiring for the night. Do you need anything?"

He appreciated her thoughtfulness but shook his head and motioned to his mug. "No, I'm fine, thank you. Mother already brought me tea."

Julia looked out the windows into the dark night. "It's beautiful up here. I can see why you enjoy your work."

He gestured for her to take a seat on the narrow bench. "You're welcome to join me for a few minutes."

Julia smiled and took a seat on the bench, the scent of her tangy lemon verbena tickling his nose. As he settled next to her, their shoulders almost touching, they looked out at the expansive night sky. The rain clouds had scattered, so the stars above poked through and twinkled like distant diamonds, and the moon radiated a silvery glimmer on the river below.

"I've always loved the night sky, but out here, it's so much darker and the stars more visible than in the city." Julia's face reflected the awe of the celestial display. "I would love to paint it one evening."

"Indeed. To me, the heavens are like a home for unspoken dreams. And the view from up here in the lighthouse is a little piece of heaven."

The measured pulse of the beam created a

soothing cadence, and faint scent of the river filled the air. Julia's close proximity set his pulse to quicken and beads of sweat to his brow.

"Do you like being a lightkeeper?"

William motioned toward the steady illumination emanating from the lens. "I find comfort in the light. It reminds me that even in the darkest of nights, there's something constant and reassuring."

Julia groaned, a long whoosh of breath following. "I wish there was something steady and inspiring for me, like this beacon is to you. But I find no comfort in the vastness of the days of uncertainty ahead of me. Instead, the emptiness of being alone shakes me to my core."

William touched her hand, patting it cautiously. "You're never alone, Julia. God said, 'I am always with you, even to the end of the world.'"

Julia blinked at his touch and shook her head. She tugged her hands into a tight ball close to her body. "I don't know that God or that peaceful feeling."

William had no response to that. It was the first time he'd ever met someone without faith like his. But Julia needed someone's help to navigate the dark and lonely waters within her. He sensed her bitterness, her hopelessness, her need of healing. But without God, how could he come to her aid?

Chapter 2

The following evening, after a dinner of chicken and dumplings, Julia took it upon herself to clear the table, urging Aunt Dee and William to indulge in their tea and spice cake in the quiet of the day's end.

The day had been one of endless monotony. She'd paced the tiny island several times before settling into reading Robert Louis Stevenson's *Treasure Island*. At least Aunt Dee had a healthy library at her disposal. Julia would probably consume the whole lot of them before summer's end.

After removing the plates and bowls, Julia joined the others at the table to enjoy the still-warm cake. She took a whiff. "I'll finish the dishes in a little while. But first, this cake smells scrumptious."

Aunt Dee chuckled. "I'm glad, and thanks for doing the dishes. It's nice to have another woman around. What do you plan to do in the fall? I fear after getting used to you being here, I will miss you terribly."

Julia sighed. "I don't know. The solicitor wouldn't allow me to stay in Granny's house—some legal thing with the will. And I gave up my place at the boarding house. By the fall, though, the lawyer should have the details settled, and I'll know what to do. Maybe I'll get a job or something."

"The good Lord will guide you, my dear. Just you wait and see."

William pushed back from the table. "I've an idea for our evening entertainment." His eyes sparked mischievously. He disappeared for a moment, then reappeared with a harmonica in hand. He winked at them, and Julia grinned in anticipation. Not the kind of entertainment she'd been used to in the city, but still . . .

A small giggle escaped Julia's lips. "What are you up to, William?"

He shrugged, took a deep breath, and started playing a lively tune. The first notes of "My Bonnie Lies over the Ocean" filled the room, and Julia burst into laughter. She clapped along to the beat, thoroughly enjoying the impromptu concert. Though it wasn't the caliber of city performances, it seemed to fit nicely here. And she was grateful for any distraction to pass the time.

William seamlessly transitioned to "Blow the Man Down," his fingers dancing across the harmonica with practiced ease. The somber man had transformed into a lively musical virtuoso right before her eyes. She swayed in her seat to the sea-inspired song, feeling as though she was on a ship bound for adventure.

"Sailing, Sailing" followed, and she closed her

eyes, imagining a gentle breeze and the sweet sound of waves. The room transformed into an imaginary sea, and William's harmonica was the captain steering them through the musical voyage.

The harmonica's melody took an unexpected turn as he played the opening notes of "O Canada!" Julia grinned, recognizing the patriotic tune from her home country. She saluted playfully and stood, while William continued respectfully, and Aunt Dee stayed seated, though she leaned in.

When William concluded his concert, slipping the harmonica into his pocket and bowing gently, his mother clapped, and Julia joined her in applauding. The island held magic in its grasp. Perhaps this was why Granny had wanted her here.

"Thank you, William." Julia's heart filled with a mingling of gratitude and nostalgia. "That was truly special, especially the last song. I learned to play 'O, Canada!' on the piano when I was young."

With a gracious smile, he acknowledged Julia's kind words. "I'm glad I could share this music with you."

For several moments, the cottage held the memory of the harmonica's enchanting tunes. In the illumination of the setting sun peeking through the windows, Julia found herself drawn to a painting on the wall—a simple riverscape that came alive with the same spirit as William's harmonica. Could the artist behind it be none other than William himself?

She pointed to the art as her pulse raced with hope that they might share an artistic passion. Perhaps that would bring a bit of solace. "William, did you create this?"

He nodded, a modest smile playing on his lips. "Yes, though I haven't painted anything in a while. I find comfort in both music and art. Each stroke of the brush or every note on the harmonica tells a story. If you ever decide to pick up playing the piano again, I'd be more than happy to accompany you."

She chuckled, a spark of inspiration and hope growing inside her. Perhaps this place wouldn't be so bad after all. "I just might take you up on that offer one day. Until then, thank you for turning an ordinary evening into a lovely concert."

Aunt Dee pecked her son's cheek, and Julia stood before making her way to the sink to do the dishes. "Good evening, William."

As she washed the dishes, the shared love of art and music gave her hope. And the unusual association between William and the memory of her deceased mother emerged through the melodies that had filled the air. Memories of her mother teaching her to play "Oh, Canada!" on the piano just days before she passed brought a lump to her throat.

But so did the loneliness that still permeated her being. Sweet as it was, a harmonica concert couldn't heal the heartbreak and emptiness she felt.

Aunt Dee returned to the kitchen and placed the kettle on the stove. "Join me for a cup of tea, dearie?"

Julia dried the last pot and tucked it on the shelf. "I'd love to." She chose two china teacups and saucers for them and sat at the table across from Aunt Dee, selecting a lovely cup with daisies on it, her senses alive to the scent of the river and the sound of the waves filling the evening air.

Aunt Dee poured them each a cup, Julia took a sip of her tea before commenting. "I've never heard a harmonica played so skillfully. Your son is quite talented."

Though weathered by years spent in the isolation and difficult work of the lighthouse, the older woman smiled at Julia with tenderness in her eyes.

"There's a story behind William taking up the instrument. You see, when he was but a boy, pleurisy paid him unwelcome visits, tormenting him over and over. The doctor, a wise old soul who knew the healing powers of both medicine and music, suggested something unique." Aunt Dee paused, a smile playing on her lips, as if the thought of such troubles held a blend of both challenge and triumph. "He recommended the harmonica, a kind of musical therapy to ward off the chronic bouts of pleurisy."

Julia furrowed her brows, curiosity growing with the steam rising from her tea and curling around her face. "How could the harmonica really help?"

Aunt Dee chuckled, the sound as winsome and welcoming as the glow of the lighthouse beam splashing light through the window. "The doctor said the deep breaths that playing it required would help William's lungs, though, at first, William struggled with it. The harmonica seemed a foreign language to him. But with time and persistence, he learned to bring melodies from that little instrument. It became his companion during the long nights when the cold winds howled and when pleurisy's pain threatened to tighten its grip. A few years ago, he added the kazoo, and that funny little instrument became his comic relief."

Julia sucked in a breath. "A kazoo? How strange."

William's mother gestured toward the small shelf in the corner, where a simple tin kazoo rested beside a well-worn harmonica. "There it is, beside the very first harmonica he played as a boy. Music became his solace, a reminder that even in the face of adversity, there's a song waiting to be played. And now, whenever the river's winds carry the sound of that harmonica out to the world, I like to think it's not just the music but the strong will of a boy who refused to let illness define him."

Julia's heart stirred with hope. Could she learn to be strong enough to fend off her trials and not let them define her as William had done? The idea that a person's will could transcend the challenges life threw at them was a powerful and new thought to her.

She sighed deeply. "I'd love to have my art do the same for me one day."

Aunt Dee's grasp on Julia's hand was both gentle and reassuring, as if she was transmitting empathy that extended beyond the physical touch. "I will pray for that, dearie."

Julia shook her head with a sense of conviction. "I don't believe in prayer. It's nothing more than knocking at a closed door—with no one behind it."

Aunt Dee responded with a quiet wisdom that had weathered the storms of doubt. "Not if you're talking to your Maker, the Creator of the universe. Julia, He is truly interested in your dreams and passions, your trials and troubles, and He cares deeply about you."

Julia masked her doubt as she glanced at William's art. "Oh, I don't know about that. I just wish the universe would send me a sign or something."

Aunt Dee's hum, filled with a lifetime of under-standing, resonated in the room. "Sometimes, God's signs are subtle, like a whisper in the wind. Or a gentle touch. Or a song. You just have to realize Who is talking and be still enough to hear Him."

Ever the skeptic, Julia raised an eyebrow. "Or maybe the universe needs to turn up the volume and make it clear."

Their shared laughter became a brief respite, easing the tension that lingered. Aunt Dee and William shared a solid foundation she lacked. But her skepticism ran deep.

As the river waves continued their ceaseless motion against the rocks outside the open kitchen window, the harmonica on the shelf and the painting on the wall offered a tiny spark of hope, bridging the gap between pain and persever-ance. Maybe her shaky foundation could find a firm footing here.

But the question resounded in her mind—was there really a God who cared? A God who would accompany her on her lonely journey?

And how could she know?

William stood by the weathered lamp room window, his gaze fixed on the distant horizon where the waves met the inky night. The steady beam of the lighthouse sprinkled fleeting shadows across the room, each one reminding him of the ghosts lingering in the corners of his mind as his chest tightened more by the moment. It couldn't be happening again, could it?

The small lantern room felt even tinier tonight, laden with the weight of a past he had desperately sought to bury beneath the responsibilities of tending to the guiding light. The melancholy hum of the lamp's machinery harmonized with the memories of a painful chapter in his life.

Louise, the one who had never truly appreciated the music that flowed through his veins or the art he attempted to create, haunted his heart. His fingers traced the edges of the harmonica in his pocket, a token of his unrequited love for the melodies that she had dismissed with a casual wave of her hand and a sour smirk of disapproval. The kazoo, too, had become a symbol of his futile attempts to bridge the gap between their worlds.

Louise, with her elegant fingers dancing gracefully across the piano keys, measured his passion for music against the standards of her own artistry. The last time he had mustered the courage to play for her, the notes had floated around like fragile promises after she begged him to stop the annoying sound. The melody he had crafted with quivering vulnerability had fallen on discriminating ears and a rejecting heart.

In the solitude of the lighthouse, the memories of those moments resurfaced like ghosts from the shadows, as they so often did. William closed his eyes, letting the haunting strains of that last rejected tune play in his mind. The comparison of his music to hers, the subtle mockery—it all stung as sharply as the sleet-laden zephyr that would seep through the cracks in the walls of the lighthouse tower when winter came crashing in. That arctic cold would freeze the river solid and send them to the mainland until the river finally thawed in spring.

During the long winters on the mainland, William merely endured the exile. Though he found part-time work at the lumber yard in Chippewa Bay, and Louise had loved him being there, he yearned for the open space and tranquil quiet of Sister Island all winter long. No, the mainland was not where he belonged, nor did he belong with Louise.

He carried the gravity of those sad memories like a ship bearing the scars of countless storms. But he didn't know how to repair the damage. Sister Lighthouse stood as an observer to his inner turmoil—a keeper of both the light that guided others and the shadows that clung to his own soul.

He coughed several times, even as deepening pain in his chest alerted him of another more insidious enemy—pleurisy's return. "Please God, no! Not again."

He struggled to draw a breath, the stabbing sensation transporting him back to a time when the ache was not just physical but emotional. The memory of his fiancée's final departure haunted his mind.

Louise had come for a visit to the island, which she rarely did. It had been a cold autumn evening when the signs of pleurisy had returned. The pain in his chest was a cruel intruder, stealing his breath and his strength. He had sought relief in the comfort of his fiancée's arm, in a love he believed could weather any storm.

But as the pain intensified, so did the strain on their relationship. The simple act of breathing became a torment, and the woman who had been his harbor of hope found herself unable to bear the weight of his affliction.

The night she had jilted him, the bitter cold—inside and outside—settled in his heart. Her eyes, once filled with affection, held pity, disgust, and fear as she uttered words that cut deeper than any pain in his chest. "I can't watch you suffer like this. When we met, you seemed so strong and vibrant." Her voice had trembled with sadness. "I didn't realize how awful your illness was, and I can't be with someone who's falling apart. Furthermore, I won't live on this island. I had always hoped you'd leave this desolate place for good and settle on the mainland with me."

And with those words, she walked away, leaving him alone in the lighthouse that had once been his sanctuary. Her footsteps against the cold metal floor echoed through the hollow space below, and the sound of that loss still reverberated in his soul.

William checked the lamp to see if it needed more oil, and his mind wandered to Julia, the woman who had recently entered his life and brought with her a refreshing breath of encouragement. Though he had sworn off all women and chosen the solitary life of Sister Island light-keeper, still . . .

Louise's disdain for his musical and artistic pursuits had left a bitter taste in his soul. Her mocking laughter had taunted him. But Julia's beaming smile and the genuine applause that she had showered upon his art and his music had revived something shriveled within.

Was Julia's kindness a mere façade, or did she truly see something in him that Louise failed to appreciate? Maybe not every woman was as judgmental and rejecting as Louise. Perhaps Julia was different—a beacon of understanding and support in a world that often seemed cold and critical.

Yet a shadow of doubt lingered. What if Julia witnessed his vulnerability, his struggle with pleurisy? Would she, like Louise, turn away in revulsion, unable to handle the less attractive aspects of his life?

The air in the lamp room felt heavy with questions as he continued to work, each small task an affirmation of his devotion. He loved his work as a keeper. The steadiness of it. The importance of protecting others. And he never wanted to leave. Not even for a woman.

In between hacking coughs, William moved about the room with deliberation and the aptitude of daily practice. He refilled the oil. But as the air became thick with the stench of it, the subtle musk of the cool river air that seeped through the open door did little to refresh him.

After he carefully adjusted the wick and checked the lamp, he retreated to the parapet, the night air unusually pleasant for mid-May but still refreshingly cool. Perhaps it would help his lungs stave off the onslaught of his chronic condition.

As he looked up at the starry sky and bright moon, the responsibility of being the keeper weighed on him, a burden he willingly shouldered, just as his father had done. Each successful night was a nod to his dedication—a devotion that went beyond the routine tasks of maintenance. Thankfully, he hadn't had a major shipping accident under his watch, and he hoped that would be his testimony well into the future. But with the rocky shoals and narrow shipping channel, danger always lurked just underneath the water's edge.

He stared at the dark waters, now still for the moment. The lighthouse was more than a beacon. More than a job. More than a friend. It was a guardian, a sentinel watching over the secrets of the mighty St. Lawrence.

Tonight, though, his thoughts were a tempest along with the storm that rose deep in his lungs. He paused, fixating on the beam that cut through the darkness, and he held back a cough. The steadiness of the light brought a sense of comfort, a reminder that even amid the uncertainty, there was order.

"Please, God. Help me be strong like this lighthouse, bright as the beam, faithful through the storms."

Chapter 3

The morning sun flooded the St. Lawrence River with a golden calm as Julia crossed the concrete break wall and set up her easel on the middle islet of Sister Island, a tiny piece of land not much bigger than Granny's library. A light breeze carried the faint scent of lilacs, and the gentle flowing of the river provided a soothing atmosphere for her artistic endeavor.

She'd longed to put her brush to the canvas from the moment she arrived on the island a week ago. Longed to do something to break the endless boredom. In the city, she'd enjoyed daily outings and parties, teas and shopping trips, and gossip-laden walks in the park. Here, no matter how gracious Aunt Dee and William were, the isolated humdrum threatened to consume her.

She had to make her own fun. With her art.

As she dipped her brush into the palette, she honed in on a lone sailboat gliding gracefully over the rippling surface of the river. Its sails, a brilliant white against the dark blue expanse, caught the sunlight just right, spreading a luminous reflection on the water.

With each stroke of her brush, Julia sought to capture the movement of the moment—the way the sailboat leaned against the wind, the play of sunlight on the water's surface, and the effortless dance of the vessel with the river's currents. The vibrant oil colors blended seamlessly onto the page, creating a scene that replicated the serenity of the St. Lawrence.

Out of the corner of her eye, she noted William's approach, but she remained engrossed in her artwork.

He squinted toward the vessel. "Are you capturing the sailboat? Mind if I sneak a peek?"

Giving a nod, she halted her brushstrokes, worry etching her thoughts as she considered William's strained and sickly appearance. His throat clearing and deep coughing concerned her even more. "Are you all right? That cough sounds pretty deep."

"I'm fine, thank you." His tone signaled avoidance of the topic. Coming around to stand behind her, he gasped, his voice raspy. "Oh, Julia. This is a masterpiece. You truly possess a remarkable gift. Keep going, Mary Cassatt."

She giggled, charmed by his assertion. "You tease. I'll never paint like any of *les trois grandes dames*, though I long to depict movement, light, and design as they did."

"Grandes dames?"

"Mary Cassatt was one of the four Impressionist women who made such an astonishing mark on the art world a few years ago."

"Of course."

A reassuring pat on her shoulder followed, and

William departed with a hushed exit, leaving her to continue her work. His compliment resonated deeply, but she tucked it away in the recesses of her mind to savor later.

As she continued painting, Julia lost herself, the world around her fading into the background. Thankfully, the sailboat seemed to be anchored for the moment, allowing her to continue her work unhindered. It became the focal point, a symbol of freedom and exploration, navigating the endless possibilities of the river.

Oh, how she wished she could voyage to places unknown, to explore the world—or even just the river! But here she was, stuck on an island. She whispered to the heavens. "I'm sorry I was such a disappointment, Granny. I'm trying to make this work here. I really am."

The sun cast its fervent embrace on the scene as she hurried to capture the vessel before it moved on. The sailboat, taking center stage on the canvas, came alive under her skilled hand. The details, from the sails to the intricate patterns in the water, crafted a narrative of a quiet journey on the St. Lawrence.

When she neared the completion of her piece of art, she stepped back to admire her work. The boat, now long gone, having sailed around the Canadian Grenadier Island, stood frozen in time, somehow evoking a sense of both tranquility and adventure. The St. Lawrence River, with its ever-changing currents, had become her muse, and Julia had captured a fleeting moment of its loveliness.

Satisfied with her creation, Julia sat back to soak in the scene before her. The painting, her first work of art on Sister Island, would not be her last. She'd make the most of this summer, if only with her artwork.

When she entered the cottage, Julia carefully propped the still-wet canvas on the kitchen table where Aunt Dee sat darning a sock. "My gift to you. To thank you for having me here."

Aunt Dee examined the work of art, studying the details carefully. "In all my days, I've never received such a treasure, Julia. Thank you, from the bottom of my heart, dearie."

The distant hum of a large freighter engine caught Julia's attention, and she peeked out the screen door, squinting against the sun, scanning the eastern expanse of the river. "It's a ship! A huge ship!"

Aunt Dee guffawed. "You'll see many of those during your summer here, but this is the first of the season. Go to the eastern edge of the island, girl, and enjoy every minute of it."

Julia hurried out the door and scurried toward the shoreline. As she passed the boathouse, William stood in the shade of it, wiping his hands on a rag.

"William! Come quick!"

A grin spread across his face as he acknowledged the approaching vessel. He cleared his throat. "Ah, a saltie! Look at the size of that ship. Quite the sight, isn't it?"

The low bellow of the ship's horn echoed through the air, announcing its presence as it approached Sister Island. Julia hurried to the tip of the main island, delight surging through her as William caught up to her. Her heart raced, and she giggled with glee.

He chuckled. "What's the hurry, Julia? That's one of those ocean-faring giants. They sail through the St. Lawrence, connecting the vast Atlantic to our Great Lakes, all summer long. Our river is a lifeline for trade up here, and now that the ice has melted, you'll also see lakers during your sojourn."

Julia nodded, enthralled at the probability of seeing such wonders throughout the summer. Perhaps she would discover more excitement here than she had thought. She compared the size of the lighthouse to the ship as it came near. "It's taller than the lighthouse."

"Yes, and longer than the entire island. Impressive, isn't it? This river is vitally important to America and Canada, Julia. It opens the heart of North America to the world."

His pride in the maritime significance of the region shone through every word he spoke, but after he coughed deeply, twice, he struggled to catch his breath.

"William, you're unwell. Perhaps you should go inside and rest?"

He waved off her comment with a scowl and fixed narrowed eyes on the vessel. She didn't need to mother him. He'd conveyed that message loud and clear. But something told her his loathing came from a deeper place.

As the ship chugged closer, Julia marveled at its sheer size. "What about those lakers you mentioned?"

"Ah, the lakers." William gestured west to where a smaller vessel bobbed along the channel. "Those ships stay in the Great Lakes and the river. They transport goods between our freshwater lakes and river ports, but they don't venture into the salty seas."

She pointed to the ship nearing them, noticing the contrast. "And the hulls? Some are wooden and some iron?"

"Exactly. You have a keen eye. We've both wooden-hulled ships and iron giants sailing through the river. Each with its own story and purpose. It's a dance of commerce and connection."

As the freighter passed Sister Island with majestic grace, the waves it created rocked the small skiff moored near the boathouse.

"It makes me feel so very small and insignificant."

William came close. "But you're neither, Julia."

Her heart skipping, she chanced a peek at him.

He cleared his throat, motioning toward the freighter. "See those stacked crates and barrels? Wheat, corn, coal, limestone, and ore—as well as general cargo—travel through these waters, fueling industries and nations. The lifeblood of the heartland flows through here, and our little island is witness to it all, standing as a guardian at the gateway of the Great Lakes."

Julia watched until the ship disappeared up the river, leaving only the fading sound of its penetrating horn.

Suddenly, she spotted a small boat caught in the tumultuous aftermath of the passing steamship. "William, look. They need help!"

Without a moment's hesitation, William ran toward the dock, and she followed, picking up her skirts and catching up with him even before he reached the boat. He untied the skiff and helped her into it.

The thrill of the adventure pulsed through her veins, her senses heightened by the urgency of the situation. The skiff wobbled in the water, but she found her balance and sat down, leaning in and ready for action. "What can I do, William?"

He coughed deeply but recovered quickly. "Keep an eye on the three of them—father, mother, and toddler, by the look of things. The water is freezing cold, since it's still May, and that little one is bound to be in the most serious peril."

William grabbed the oars, and she never took her eyes off the family. Their boat was floundering, one end tilting perilously close to the water.

"Hurry, William. They're tipping."

As he rowed toward the distressed vessel, the wind carried the passengers' cries for help—the desperate pleas of a couple, their voices strained with worry, and the frightened whimpering of a toddler. The listing vessel told the tale of a struggle against the unforgiving current and wake of the ship. If only she were a praying woman . . .

Could they make it in time? A mixture of fear and worry set her nerves on edge.

Though William coughed repeatedly, his face ghostly white, he rowed with amazing speed, the boat slicing through the water and quickly closing the gap.

Julia's heart raced as she beheld the couple desperately clinging to the side of the partially submerged boat, their faces etched with panic and hope, trying to keep the tiny child dry and safe. "William, we need to get them out of there, and quickly!"

The tiny toddler, clad in a bulky life jacket, was held tightly by the frightened mother. Dark curls clung to his teary face as he now howled his horror.

William slowed the skiff, concern etched on his face. "Almost there. But be careful. Panicked people can endanger us, tipping our boat in an attempt to seek safety. I'll steady the boat while you pull them in. Baby first."

William maneuvered the skiff alongside the listing boat and steadied it while she grabbed the flailing child, wide-eyed and trembling, from his mother's arms and set him at her own feet. The child clung to her legs and cried, "Mama!" over and over, but he didn't move.

After much maneuvering, Julia tugged the woman into the boat, and she quickly helped Julia pull her husband into the skiff. She sighed deeply. How rewarding that she'd helped bring three souls to safety.

Julia picked up the child and handed him to his mother. "Easy now, little one. You're safe."

The thin, soggy mother whimpered. "Thank you. Thank you so much." She hugged the child to her chest, enfolding him in the warmth of her body, and continued to cry softly.

William nodded to them. "You're welcome. Where to?"

With chattering teeth, the short, balding man pointed to a cottage on an island near the mainland, a few hundred yards from where they were. "My father's place is just there, on Hemlock Island."

William turned the rowboat toward the cottage, and as they neared, the couple embraced their child, their expressions a brew of exhaustion and gratitude. Tears glistened in their eyes as they stepped onto the riverbank, the peril of their journey now a bystander to the kindness of the river community.

The father held out his hand. "Thank you, folks. We're forever in your debt."

William waved off his words. "Just glad you're safe. Godspeed."

Julia waved goodbye, her chest constricting. Both an unpredictable charm and a somber responsibility came with living near the St. Lawrence. The rescue, though heart-pounding, had shown her courage, camaraderie, and the unwavering spirit of William—and she guessed, of all who called the river their home. The urgency of the situation gave way to a sense of accomplishment as the skiff made its way toward the safety of the Sister Island. Her first great adventure at the lighthouse. It was far more thrilling than the fanciest party back home.

But more dangerous too.

William wiped his brow. "That was too close for comfort. I'm glad you saw them, Julia. Well done!"

He smiled, but then he broke into another series of alarming coughs, and all the way back to the lighthouse, the poor man hacked and coughed and gasped for breath.

She stole glances at him and struggled to keep from taking the oars. Was he coming down with something? Or was something more serious wrong?

In his small, dimly lit bedroom, William lay in bed, his chest weighted with pain. The steady pulse of the river crept in through the open window and the flickering glow of the oil lamp splashed eerie shadows on the walls, failing to bring peace like it usually did. Nothing helped when he felt like this.

The river, once a companion during his solitary pain-filled nights, now carried a cruel chill that permeated the room, billowing the curtains like ghosts. He'd hoped the fresh air might help, but it didn't. Every breath he took was a struggle, a raspy wheeze that crackled through the silence of the room. The exertion of the rescue hadn't helped his condition one bit.

His once-steady hands trembled as he attempted to reach for the glass of water on the bedside table. Beads of sweat dotted his forehead, and his breaths came in shallow gasps. The onset of pleurisy had stolen the air from his lungs, leaving him desperate for relief.

The distant sound of waves crashing against the rocks mocked him, a reminder of the vast expanse he'd not be able to effectively surveil in his weakened state. Worse, he couldn't do his job, leaving it up to his mother to light the lamp. And while she was perfectly capable of filling in for him, he hated to feel like a weak and inept failure.

A delicate knock on the door tore him from his self-chastisement. Julia entered, a gentle smile on her face and a book in her hand. "Your mother is tending the light, so I've come to attend you."

Unlike Louise's, Julia's tone and expression held only kindness and compassion. Not a hint of fear or exasperation such as he'd seen in his former fiancée. Perhaps Julia wouldn't judge his weakness or reject him for his frailties.

Though he longed to breathe the crisp, fresh air that had been his ally for years, now it only fueled the fire in his chest. He cleared his throat, hoping he wouldn't cough. "Would you please lower the windows? There's a cold wind tonight."

Julia nodded, and quick as a wink, she shut one and lowered the other so that only the slightest puff of wind mingled with the room's air—and the scent of her lemon verbena. "That should help. Shall I read to you? Or would you rather rest? Either way, I'm here for whatever you need. I'll be by your side until you're fit as a fiddle."

"Thank you, Julia. I should rest." His voice came out as a raspy whisper, so he turned his head toward the wall, distressed that she observed his infirmity.

"That's fine. I brought *Treasure Island* to read."

As he lay there in the quiet hearing only the turn of a page or the creak of the chair Julia sat in, his body wracked with pain, each breath continued to be a struggle against the sharp sting in his chest. Pleurisy was a cruel guest that lingered in his lungs, revisiting him a few times every year since he was a boy. He was helpless under its power.

He peeked at Julia, and a soft exhale escaped him. The woman before him reminded him of a masterpiece crafted with strokes of ginger hues. Her lively eyes sparkled with an inner light as they scanned the page of her book, even as a sadness belied her heartache. The strange but alluring combination intrigued him.

But it was more than her physical charm that captured his attention. It was the delight she'd exhibited during the rescue and the kind and caring way she helped the family. How she jumped in to assist his mother around the cottage. And now, as if adding another layer to her, she displayed a new depth in her character—a selfless devotion to him that touched his soul.

Yet something deeper than her grief lurked beneath the surface. An emptiness? A loneliness? A longing for more? She'd spoken of not knowing God. Perhaps that was it. If so, he needed to guard his heart even more carefully. He couldn't be entangled with someone who lacked the faith he held dear even though she'd visited his dreams more than once.

As if she was reading his thoughts, Julia looked

up from her book, a smidgen of surprise—or was it alarm?—passing through her eyes. "Can I help?"

Before he could answer, Julia set aside her book, stood, and moved gracefully toward him, her footsteps almost silent against the softly creaking floorboards. Her presence quickened his heartrate and acted as a balm to the ache in William's body. With a light touch, she adjusted the pillows behind him, the dainty silver bracelet she often wore brushing against his cheek.

She glanced at it and frowned. "Sorry. Rest, William." Her calm voice eased the tension in his chest. "I'll make some hot tea and add plenty of honey. It might help."

He nodded weakly, and she smiled sweetly before leaving the room. He marveled at her benevolence, an understanding of the depth of his suffering clear in her every gesture.

When she returned with the tea, he gratefully sipped the soothing drink. Julia moved her chair and sat beside him, her compassion unwavering. "I'm sorry you're not feeling well."

He swallowed the lump in his throat. "Thanks, Julia. For everything."

Once again, the stark contrast between Julia and his former fiancée was not lost to him. Louise had been cold and heartless during his illness, far different from Julia's caring and genuine concern.

William's mother knocked and entered the room,

her worried glance moving between Julia and himself as she came close and tenderly felt his forehead. "I've lit the lamp just fine, son. It's a calm, clear night, so there should be no trouble, but I'll stay at the post and sleep in the morning. There's no need for you to worry. You just concentrate on getting well."

Mother turned to Julia and hugged her. "Thank you for being here. Your presence is providential. He hasn't had one of these bouts for almost a year, so I'm grateful you're willing to help."

Julia smiled, her empathy constricting his lungs even more. "I'm happy to assist in any way I can. Really."

When his mother left the room, an uncomfortable silence took her place. Mother would never have left him alone with Louise, even for a moment. She never liked the woman, never trusted her. But Julia? She treated Julia like her own daughter.

"Thank you, Julia," he whispered, his voice hoarse as a frog's. "Your kindness means more to me than you can imagine."

Meeting his gaze with a gracious smile, Julia placed her hand on his. "It's the least I can do, William. You're not alone in this trial. I'm here for you."

Perhaps not every woman was as heartless as Louise. As he lay there, memories of storms weathered and ships guided bolstered him, but this ailment was worse than the greatest tempest. Though he was grateful for his mother's and Julia's help, what if the lighthouse inspector came and saw him like this? Would he lose his position? Lightkeeping was his calling, his life's work. Without being lightkeeper of Sister Island like his father, who was he?

In the quiet moments between painful breaths, his thoughts drifted to the beam of light sweeping across the darkness outside. Julia was quickly becoming a beacon of hope to him. Yet her words in the lantern room rushed back to haunt him. *I don't know that God or that feeling.*

She didn't believe as he did. He couldn't forget that. And he could not be marooned by another emotional shipwreck.

Chapter 4

Julia had fretted over William for days. It had taken him a full week to recover, poor man. During that time, he had been aloof and standoffish—and often in a foul mood. Since he'd risen from his sickbed, he'd kept her at arm's length, putting up an impenetrable defensive wall. But why?

She wanted to know, so she found William by the water, a fishing rod in one hand, his attention focused on the gentle ripples that danced on the surface around the line he'd cast.

She approached quietly, not wanting to disturb the serenity of the scene, and barely whispered her greeting, hoping to soothe the strain between them. "Good evening, William. I hope you can catch something before heading up to the light. Your mother sent me to give you this mug of tea."

"Thank you." He glanced at the slowly sinking sun and took the mug and sipped before setting it on a flat rock near him. "I still have thirty minutes or so, and that should be enough. This time of day is best for fishing. And sunrise too."

His voice still had a touch of raspiness in it, and his tone suggested a jumble of annoyance and tranquility, creating a puzzling undercurrent.

Would an illness cause that, or was there something deeper?

She turned her attention to marvel at the loveliness unfolding before her. It really was beautiful here.

The air filled her senses with the soothing symphony of nature—the soft lapping of the water, the distant chirping of birds, and the occasional rustle of leaves in the wind. The river stretched as far as she could see in all directions, its water radiating the shades of the sleepy sun. Each island reminded her of Granny's jewels, scattered across the surface of the St. Lawrence River.

The sight never got old, just as William had said.

The gentle breeze flitted around her, tugging at her hair as she stood next to William. She pulled an old photograph from her pocket and cradled it in her hands. The image depicted a cherished memory of her granny, frozen in amber nostalgia. Though it was merely a portrait of Granny, Julia imagined herself fastening the pearls around her neck—a daily ritual that held the essence of that timeless bond.

The pearls, luminous and delicate, captured the very spirit of those quiet afternoons spent together. Granny's hands, weathered by time and no longer able to manage the delicate clasp, held comfort that transcended time.

As Julia closed her eyes, she could almost hear the clinking of the costly gems, a melody that accompanied their shared moments. The daily habit was more than simply adorning Granny with jewelry. The ritual was a special moment of closeness, a bridge between generations.

"A penny for your thoughts?" William peeked over her shoulder at the photograph. "Is that your grandmother?"

"It is. Your mother and she were friends and pen pals, but you never met her?"

William cleared his throat. "I rarely joined Mother for her Canadian jaunts. Especially because she was visiting her 'old friends,' as she called them, and didn't seem to want a busy little boy about them." A chuckle escaped his lips as he sipped his tea. "Sorry, I meant no disrespect."

"None taken."

Julia stood next to William as he fished, the sun soon dipping lower in the sky and spreading a golden tone on the scene. A memory came alive in Julia's mind—the aroma of Granny's favorite tea, the gentle laughter that wafted through the air, and the pearls against the older woman's neck. Her wrinkled, comforting hands lifting a shaky teacup.

She ran a finger over the photograph. "I wish I had Granny's pearls. She wore them every day. They made her look regal. Special."

William's brow furrowed. "Where did they go?"

She shrugged. "I don't know. They weren't among her things after she passed."

With a bittersweet smile, Julia scanned the photograph still in her hands. The wind continued to play with her hair, as if Granny's spirit lingered in it, whispering tales of the past.

The ritual of fastening the necklace and sipping tea had become a treasured memory, moments that occupied a prominent place in the gallery of her heart, a reminder that some bonds are as enduring as the gems Granny had worn with such grace.

If she survived the wretched summer, hopefully, she'd find those pearls. But surely, her reluctant agreement to live on the island was about more than that . . .

William yanked on the line. "I've got something. A hefty catch."

With effort, he reeled in a large carp.

Julia marveled at the creature. "It must weigh fifty pounds."

He removed the hook from its mouth and held it up. "More like thirty, but he's no good for eating."

William released the fish back into the river and baited his hook. He didn't seem interested in talking, so instead, she surveyed her surroundings again.

The half-dozen trees on Sister Island stood tall and proud, though a little bent by the westerly winds that blew constantly. Bullfrogs croaked. Mosquitoes, butterflies, dragonflies, and other bugs flitted around. Seagulls squawked and circled. For a moment, a magnificent blue heron stopped on the island. For a rest? Food? Perhaps its mate nested nearby.

"I thought staying on an island would be unbearably boring, that my surroundings would never change, and that I'd miss the city life more than I do." Her eyes traced the patterns of sunlight playing on the water. "But the river and everything around it is always changing, moving, breathing. Father was right. Nature is truly glorious, isn't it, William?"

He glanced at her, a frown forming on his lips. "There is a certain peace that comes with being surrounded by God's creation. A reminder of something—or Someone—greater than ourselves."

She shrugged. "Oh, I don't know about that. The simplicity of moments like these, the way the world continues to evolve all on its own with no need of our interference—it's awe-inspiring."

William didn't respond to her comment, but a tiny groan escaped his lips.

"What a spectacle these Thousand Islands are, cut by the glaciers so long ago. My father always talked about the unhurried movement of time. I can almost feel the cold, looking at all this." She gave an expressive shiver. "Some of these islands are no more than a rocky outcropping, while others host dense forests like Grenadier. I feel inspired just being here. I wonder if the spiritual experience of it was why Granny bid me to sojourn here."

A tangle of perplexity and concern played on his face. "Perhaps the reason is deeper than that, Julia. Moments like these make me appreciate the wonders of God's creation. The splendor we see is a reflection of the Creator who made it all. A reminder of His love and care for us."

She pasted on a smile, acknowledging his perspective. "Don't you find spirituality in the sanctity of nature itself? I think that nature is sacred in its own right, not because of some religious being, but simply for what it is."

William stared at her with a furrowed brow. "I appreciate the beauty of nature, Julia, but I believe it's all an expression of God's creativity and majesty. He is the Creator of everything we see, and His creation points to Him."

She raised an eyebrow, irritation rising. "But William, isn't the idea of God and the Bible a bit old-fashioned? My father taught me to find meaning and awe in the intricate web of life itself, in the delicate balance of nature, without the need for a divine presence."

William leaned in close to her, his eyes sincere. "God is not old-fashioned. He is timeless, and His teachings provide us with a moral compass. And the Bible isn't just a book, Julia. It is truth.

It holds the best counsel for understanding our purpose and finding closeness to God. Moreover, His creation is for us to enjoy, not to worship."

Julia huffed. She plunged her grandmother's photograph into her pocket and folded her arms across her chest. Her pulse quickened, and she shifted from one foot to the other.

He sounded like her mother, a Bible-thumping church-goer who argued and demeaned her father for his progressive views. Views she held dear. "On the contrary, William. I find meaning in appreciating the interconnectedness of all living things. Nature, to me, is its own sacred entity, and I don't need the concept of God to find wonder and meaning."

William frowned, a thoughtful expression on his face. "I hope your journey to understanding the world here and beyond will lead you to the truth of who God is. God is the source of everything, Julia, and the Bible is the best guide to navigating our complex existence."

Julia gasped. "That's not what my father taught me. My truth may not be the same as yours, but I hope you'll respect it."

He swallowed, snapping off a half nod. "I best be lighting the lamp. I hope you have a good evening and will find this summer to be a life-changing one. Good night." William's tone revealed neither hope nor good will. Instead, it sounded more like judgment. Like Mother's.

As the sun dipped lower, distributing longer shadows across the island, William gathered his fishing equipment and his pail of four fish, while Julia lingered on the shore.

"Good evening, William." Her tone sounded short. Defensive.

How dare he try and cram his religion down her throat? At least Aunt Dee was subtle about her beliefs.

But what if there really was more to this world than nature alone, as Father had said? What if Mother was right?

What if William was?

William entered the lamp room, clutching his Bible close. His heart weighed heavily as he lit the lamp. He had never met a person who thought like Julia did, let alone, at the same time, experienced such a strong attraction to an enchanting woman. Even Louise's magnetism paled in the shadow of Julia's luminous pull. A tug he had best avoid.

The quiet of the lamp room and the security of the lighthouse's powerful presence gave him the fortitude to chase down his thoughts. He murmured to God, as he often did on duty. "Guide me, Lord. Help me think through this conundrum and make sense of it all."

The broken betrothal and subsequent rejection still stung, even these many months later. And the temptation of seeking refuge in Julia's affections, with her captivating charm and artistic spirit, intensified within him. Her vibrant spirit and intriguing views of the world formed a magical picture that enticed him, and resultant nervous energy coursed through his veins as he speculated on what succumbing to them would mean.

He needed a distraction, so he dove into his nightly rituals, cleaning the smudges from the lightroom windows and sweeping away gnats and other bugs that had made their way in. The routine was familiar, a comforting activity that allowed his mind to wander. But thoughts of Julia returned like a persistent tune, refusing to be pushed to the background.

The brass gleamed under his attentive hands as he polished it, each stroke mimicking the inner turmoil he grappled with. The idea of a deeper friendship with Julia beckoned, a chance to delve safely into the depths of who she was, to understand her intricacies and perspectives— without any romantic and complicated entanglements.

Yet in the quiet of the room, he confronted the danger of succumbing to the temptation lurking beneath the surface. Conflict brewed within him. He was a man torn between the desire to explore a fondness for Julia and the imperative to protect and guard his heart.

"No!" His whisper became a mantra against

the rising tide of temptation. "I must build walls, high and impenetrable. Guard my heart against the allure of her."

The vulnerability of opening up to Julia, of allowing her into the sacred chambers of his heart, threatened the stability he sought. As he finished his tasks in the lamp room, he embraced the awareness that the walls he had to erect were not only physical but also emotional—a fortress to shield him from the potential complexities of a relationship with Julia.

Indeed, after Louise, he should have learned his lesson, but here he was contemplating an even more dangerous alliance. Louise gave up on her commitment to him due to illness and the prospect of isolation, but could he fathom compromising his beliefs for Julia?

The silent sweep of the light created a comforting and intimate atmosphere that invited even deeper introspection. His gaze fell on the well-worn pages of his father's Bible, its leather cover bearing the imprints of countless hours of contemplation both of his father and himself.

The absence of his father's wisdom and sturdy guidance left an unmistakable void in his life. In the aftermath of Louise's departure, the older man had been a steadfast anchor for William's shattered heart. His father had provided more than just advice—he'd been a wellspring of wisdom from a higher perspective, a source of comfort grounded in faith, and a beacon of hope for the uncertain future. Mere months later, William had lost him. Now he grappled with that profound sense of loss. Who could fill the void and offer counsel in the way his father once had?

The ache for paternal guidance lingered, a quiet longing for the reassuring voice that had steered him through the storms of life. His mother, while compassionate and loving, couldn't completely step into the shoes of the man who had been both a pillar of strength and a fountain of wisdom. And there were limits to what he could confide in her.

William opened the Bible and traced the lines of Scripture with his fingertips. What an important role faith played in relationships. This book held stories of love, devotion, and the enduring strength founded on unwavering faith. Each passage whispered the age-old truths that bound hearts together, transcending the earthly boundaries of circumstance and challenge.

Why had Julia rejected such precious claims? She'd mentioned her father's alternative beliefs and her adherence to them, but how could she believe in nothing but the natural world? It didn't make sense.

What he believed wasn't merely a set of rules but a binding force that weathered the worst storms. A compass to navigate the complexities of human interaction. Faith wasn't confined to the sacred verses alone. No. Faith served as a guiding light, illuminating the path toward understanding, compassion, and shared values.

His mind drifted between the biblical narratives and the unfolding chapters of his own life.

Though Louise had a similar faith to his, hers proved shallow in the shadow of pleurisy and had become futile in the face of life-altering decisions. But faith was meant to be a dynamic force, adapting to the nuances of each unique experience. What if Julia's faith was nonexistent? What was he to do with that?

William closed the Bible with a sense of newfound clarity. Faith was the very foundation that should uphold love and commitment. It created enduring compatibility.

And Julia's lack of it put a roadblock to even considering a future with her.

Thankfully, she would only be here for the summer, and then she'd be gone. Back to her city life. And the temptation would pass. In that knowledge, William embraced the somber decision to retreat behind the safety of protective walls and shield himself from the potential future that might have unfolded in the arms of Julia.

Yet maintaining emotional distance would be a challenge. On this tiny island with only the three of them—well, it was impossible to not have contact with her. That would prove daunting.

He assessed his surroundings. All secure for

the moment. He'd need more fuel for the night ahead, both kerosene for the lamp and coffee for him.

He climbed down the ladder and narrow staircase and headed for the kitchen.

Mother and Julia were still up, chattering away at the kitchen table. His mother was speaking. "I've only been to Brockville twice but found it a lively town, and your granny had a lovely home."

William stopped in the dining room, staying just out of sight, and listened.

"Brockville holds its history in every brick and cobblestone." Julia's voice carried a nostalgic tone. "It was once a bustling hub for trade and commerce, with parties, people, and stores galore. The river brought prosperity to our little town, but I paid it no heed. I enjoyed the shopping and fancied my time with friends. I never considered the river as important, though I lived near it all my life." Her voice rose as she continued. "Granny said that Brockville was known as the 'City of the Thousand Islands' back in her day. I think that title speaks to the natural beauty that surrounds it. The Thousand Islands still draws artists, poets, and dreamers to our quaint town, and that's what I like the most."

A pause in the conversation bid William to join them. "Good evening, ladies. I thought it a good time to get more fuel for the lamp and me. Don't let me interrupt you."

His mother smiled. "Sit for a moment, son. It's a quiet night on the river."

He snapped a glance at Julia, and his heart stirred. If only . . .

He poured a cup of coffee and sat beside his mother.

Julia acknowledged him with a bright smile, playing with her bracelet absentmindedly. "My mother's family arrived in Brockville in the 1850s due to the Irish Potato Famine. Though they fared better than most of the Irish, they sought a new beginning, and the charm of the town captured them. The community welcomed them with open arms, she said, and they found rest in the simple life by the river."

Until now, she had barely mentioned her parents. Maybe now he could understand them better, and by extension, her. "And your father?"

She smiled and wet her lips with her tongue. "His family had been there for more than a decade, building a thriving timber business and making quite a name for themselves. Father was an architect and important on the city council. Thanks to him and other progressive thinkers, Brockville evolved over the years, from gas lamps to electric lights from horse-drawn carriages to soon expecting the first automobiles. And I miss him."

Mother placed a hand on Julia's. "This is a season of change for you, Julia. Embrace it and let it do its work."

William shifted in his seat, struggling to keep at bay his attraction to her. He stood to leave them be.

Mother has good advice. For both of us.

Chapter 5

The cozy parlor—illuminated by the oil lamp and the gentle crackling of wood in the fireplace—finally seemed safe enough after three days of tension following her disagreement with William about the importance of the natural world. Julia joined him there as he read the paper for a few minutes before heading up to light the lamp.

The scent of the river filled the air as it blew in through the open parlor window. She sat on the faded settee next to Aunt Dee, whose fingers deftly worked her needles as she sat close to the oil lamp, knitting as she always did. Well, knitted, crocheted, darned, or tatted—whatever kept her fingers moving.

Julia opened her book. "Dishes done and put away. I think I shall read a bit."

William looked up from his newspaper. "What are you reading?"

She grinned, lifting her book to show him the cover. "*Walden* by Henry David Thoreau. It's my third reading of it."

William raised an eyebrow, a smirk playing on his lips. "Sounds like a real page-turner."

She shot him a playful glare. "Oh, come on! It's a masterpiece."

He chuckled, but his furrowed brow exposed misgiving. "I'm teasing. I've heard that it's a classic."

"Thoreau's journey into the woods, living deliberately with nature as his guide and finding life's meaning—it's profound."

"I see. So what specifically has you diving into it for the third time?"

She leaned back, thoughts igniting with enthusiasm. "Father gave it to me just before he passed. It was his favorite too. There's something about Thoreau's words that resonates with me. His quest for a meaningful life really speaks to my soul. It's as though he's saying, 'forget all the external chaos and all the other ideas about life, and find your own truth within yourself and in the beauty of nature.' "

William nodded, though it struck her that he might be feigning seriousness. "Ah, the pursuit of inner peace. Deep stuff."

His disapproval wouldn't dissuade her of her father's teachings that easily. Perhaps she could persuade *him*. "Absolutely! You should read it. It might just change your perspective on life. It's like a roadmap to authenticity, you know?" She fidgeted with her book, her hands sweeping over the cover. The tension in the room shattered the tenuous peace. Just when she thought all that God talk was put to rest. . . .

William leaned back in his chair, the wooden

frame creaking slightly beneath him. He seemed oblivious to the tension settling between them. "God's word holds the key to authenticity." His eyes brightened with fervor. "That's the real roadmap to discovering who you truly are."

She mustered a tight-lipped smile, attempting to keep her growing frustration from her voice. "I respect your beliefs, but not everyone finds solace in religion. Some believe in the power within themselves, in embracing their uniqueness without relying on an external force."

His eyes softened, acknowledging the delicate balance of their conversation. "Julia, I'm not trying to impose my beliefs on you. I just genuinely believe that there's a divine purpose for each of us, one that brings true fulfillment and authenticity."

She sighed, her shoulders slumping. "I understand, William. But my belief is in the journey of self-discovery, in the messy process of becoming who I want to be. No offense, but I don't need a deity to guide me."

Aunt Dee set her work on her lap and patted the well-worn Bible on the table next to her, drawing attention to it. She smiled at Julia, grasping her hand gently. "Julia, dear, you're welcome to use my Bible anytime you like. It's always here, just waiting to be read. Perhaps it would help you understand William's perspective. And mine." Her voice was kind and inviting, not a hint of judgment.

Julia frowned, but she met Aunt Dee's gaze. "Thank you. I appreciate your generosity, but I must respectfully decline."

The older woman's brows furrowed in gentle confusion. "My dear, is there a specific reason you won't even explore the subject?"

She bit her lip while she chose her words carefully. She glanced at Aunt Dee and then at William. She had to make them understand. "I believe that nature, in all its diversity and wonder, is sufficient to elicit the intellectual and emotional responses associated with a spiritual experience. I find enjoyment and inspiration in the world around us."

Aunt Dee nodded, her eyes showing a combination of understanding and concern. "But, my dear, faith in God can bring immense comfort and guidance beyond our surroundings."

The air hung heavy with the clash of incompatible ideologies. Was Aunt Dee ganging up on her too?

Julia slipped her hand from the older woman's and clasped hers together. "I respect your beliefs, and I'm grateful for your kindness. However, I've come to abandon the superstition of a higher power, as my father did. I believe in the inherent goodness of humanity and the potential that exists within the natural world. That, to me, is enough."

Aunt Dee sighed, a fusion of sadness and

acceptance in her eyes. "Everyone has their own path of faith to walk. I'm here if you ever feel the need for spiritual guidance."

Julia smiled as tenderly as she could, but tears threatened to master her. Would this be a wedge between them for the rest of the summer? "Thank you. Your kindness means a lot to me, and I value our friendship regardless of our varying beliefs."

As she tried to focus on the words in her book, she couldn't escape the unspoken differences that hovered in the air. The room, usually a place of comfort, of shared stories and laughter, now crackled with unspoken strain. The rhythmic clacking of Aunt Dee's knitting needles became a staccato beat, punctuating the uneasy silence.

William folded his newspaper with a deliberate snap, breaking the quiet in a way that felt intrusive. He cleared his throat, sneaking a subtle glance at both Julia and his mother, as if searching for a bridge to mend the gap that had formed.

Aunt Dee, ever the peacemaker, let out another sigh, this one tinged with a hint of regret. She set her knitting aside and rested her hands on her lap. "Julia, my dear, I hope you understand that our differences in faith don't change how much I care about you. On this island, we are family, and that's a bond stronger than any disagreement."

Julia nodded, appreciating Aunt Dee's attempt to soothe the palpable discomfort. "I know, and

I cherish our bond too. It's just . . . sometimes, it feels as though we're standing on opposite shores, trying to bridge a gap that keeps widening."

Aunt Dee's smile radiated love, as if understanding the pain in Julia's words. "Faith is a journey, dear. It has many twists and turns, and sometimes, paths diverge. But love remains constant. We may not see eye to eye on everything, but that doesn't diminish the love I have for you."

The room, caught in the crossfire of conflicting emotions, seemed to exhale as Aunt Dee spoke. Julia managed a small, grateful smile and blinked back a tear.

William acknowledged the fragile truce by folding his newspaper once more, gently this time. As he set it aside, it became a wordless gesture of solidarity. "I agree with Mother. We're all on a spiritual journey, Julia. I have my own heartaches and questions that test my faith. The loss of Father and . . ."

His eyes grew wide as if he hadn't meant to uncover his pain. He pasted his lips together.

Aunt Dee nodded appreciatively at his words. The air in the room lightened, the tension dissipating further.

Julia looked at William with fresh understanding. Beneath their differing beliefs, they all grappled with their own struggles. "I appreciate your honesty, William. It takes strength to open up about your doubts and pain. We may choose different foundations, but the shared experience of the struggle is something we can connect on."

He gave a faint smile. "Thank you, Julia. It's not always easy to admit when you're wrestling with your beliefs. But in the end, I find peace in the fact that God understands our struggles and is with us in them."

Aunt Dee hummed, her voice gentle yet firm. "And, my dear Julia, I hope you know that regardless of where your path leads, you're never alone. The power of faith lies not only in its certainty but also in the journey of seeking and questioning."

As they settled into a contemplative quiet, the discomfort was replaced with an unspoken understanding. William picked up his newspaper, but this time, instead of the loud rustling of pages, he read with a quieter reverence. Julia closed her book for a moment, her thoughts lingering on the shared vulnerability in the room.

In the quiet reconciliation, her tears dried, the blurred words in her book coming into focus once more. But the book, once dear to her, seemed to be losing its charm, the words hollow and heady.

Where was the heart?

The next morning, William stood at the edge of the dock, steadying the side of a sturdy wooden skiff with his strong grip. The sun splattered gemstones over the still waters of the St. Lawrence River as he looked over his shoulder and grinned at Julia, who stood nervously beside him. "All right, Julia, it's time to learn the art of rowing."

Julia eyed the skiff with obvious apprehension. "I've never done this before, William. What if I capsize the boat?"

He chuckled. "Don't you worry, Julia. I've been rowing these waters since I was a boy, and I won't let anything happen to you. Now, step into the boat, and I'll show you the ropes."

She took a deep breath as if summoning her courage and stepped into the skiff, taking the stern seat. The boat swayed under her weight, making her grip the sides for stability.

He untied the boat, pushed it away from the dock, and maneuvered the oars through the water. The splash of liquid against the boat created a soothing melody that emulated the peaceful surroundings. His muscles responded with enthusiasm and determination as he effortlessly guided the boat forward.

"See, it's all about finding that perfect balance between strength and skill." He patted the seat beside him. Had she noticed the anticipation he couldn't keep from leaking into his tone? "Now, you give it a try."

Julia tentatively traded seats, taking the middle one and grasping the oars. The skiff rocked slightly, but William steadied it with a shift of his weight as he took the seat at the stern, eager to coach her.

With a deep breath, she attempted to mimic his movements, the boat responding with a subtle sway. At first, the process proved elusive, the oars clumsily dipping into the water with irregular splashes and the craft going nowhere.

He needed to encourage her. "Don't worry. You'll get it. Let's work on coordinating the oars. Keep them parallel to each other. Use your mid-section's muscles to power the stroke."

He demonstrated, pretending to row. Julia tried again. Though the boat continued to wobble, he remained patient, offering guidance and encouragement. He'd never taught anyone, well, anything, so this was a brand-new experience for him too.

"Imagine you're waltzing with the water." He gestured through the air to emphasize the alliance between the rower and the waves beneath.

Slowly but surely, Julia found her cadence. Finally, the oars created synchronized movements that mimicked his earlier demonstration.

As they rowed farther from the dock, Julia's nervous frown turned into an accomplished smile. With each stroke, she became more adept until the boat glided smoothly through the serene expanse.

Julia threw her head back and laughed heartily. "I've been in boats dozens of times, probably more, but I never realized the skill it takes to row smoothly. This is a lot of fun, and rewarding too. Thank you for teaching me, William."

He chuckled, pleased by her enjoyment of it. Her eyes sparkled in the sunshine. "You're a quick learner. Well done! May I ask you a favor, please?"

She nodded. "Of course."

The air crackled with his unspoken request as he sat there, caught in the crossroads of hesitation. A fleeting idea, like a whisper in the wind, crossed his mind. They hovered on a boundary between friendship and something more seemed delicate, like a fragile thread he feared might snap at any moment. Especially after last night. Should he take such a step?

Julia sat there, a mere arm's length away, her presence enveloping him with an intensity that went beyond the heat of the sun's rays. He glanced at her, searching for any clue in the depths of her eyes. The fear of complicating their growing friendship tumbled in his thoughts, yet the desire for a deeper closeness urged him forward.

He cleared his throat. "May I call you 'Gingersnap'? Every time I look into your beautiful eyes, they remind me of my favorite cookie."

Julia guffawed. "My father nicknamed me that—for that very reason. Aye, I'd be honored, sir." As she continued to row, her enormous grin confirmed the camaraderie that enveloped them.

He blew out a breath, pleased the moniker was a blessing to her—and nothing more.

The river shone with the colors of the rising sun, creating a breathtaking scene around them. Seagulls cried overhead, and the gentle lapping of the water against the skiff provided soothing music that seemed to float between them. He had bridged a bit of the gap, and it felt good.

A proud smile crossed his face. "See, Julia? You're a natural. You feel the rhythm, and before you know it, you're gliding along with the currents. Shall I take over for a while?"

She nodded, and they switched places. As they continued circumnavigating Sister Island, William shared stories of the river—of its history, the wildlife that called it home, and the countless adventures he'd had on its waters.

He gestured toward the lighthouse. "They built the lighthouse back in 1870 to mark a dangerous shoal on the Canadian side of the shipping channel. But soon after the light was commissioned, they shifted the shipping channel to the American side. Big ships, deep waters—you know how it goes. And to make that happen, they had to blast through the bedrock, making way for an alternative path." A hint of sadness filled his thoughts as he continued. "It was a peculiar twist of fate, really. When they were drilling holes and placing dynamite in the channel to carve a passage for the ships, tragedy struck. Lightning hit the drilling barge, and it set off a tremendous explosion."

Julia gasped. "No! Was anyone hurt?"

He paused, his tone affirming the import of the story. "Eleven crew members lost their lives that day. A stark reminder of the risks they faced, and the challenges they overcame to shape this waterway. Sister Island Lighthouse bears witness to the sacrifice made in the name of progress."

"Such a tragedy, and such a sacrifice." Julia sighed. "All those families affected by the accident. They would never be the same."

"True, but on a brighter note, there have been boatloads of successful rescues in these waters as well. Just days before my father died last summer, he and I had an encounter with a grandfather and young grandson out on the water. They snagged on a shoal, and the skiff took a bad hit."

Julia's eyes widened. "Were they okay? What happened?"

He nodded, allowing a reassuring smile to play on his lips. "They were fine, thanks to a bit of quick thinking from my father."

He recounted the details of the rescue—the frantic calls for help, the sinking skiff, and the grandfather and grandson desperately bailing out the water. "The poor skiff had a hole punched right through the hull. They were taking on water fast, and the grandfather seemed to be having angina of the heart."

As he spoke, Julia glanced down at their boat's hull as the gravity of the situation sank in. "Like the family's boat. It must have been terrifying for them. Was he okay?"

William leaned closer, the memory speeding up his pulse. "It was touch and go for a bit, but we managed to get them safely to shore and to a doctor, and he recovered. The river can be unpredictable, and sometimes folks find themselves in a bit of trouble. But that's what community is all about—looking out for each other, lending a helping hand when it's needed."

By the time they returned to the dock, Julia stepped out of the skiff, a new confidence in her step. "Thank you, William. I never thought rowing could be so magical."

William winked. "The river has a way of teaching us things we never knew we needed to learn, Gingersnap. Now, how about we celebrate with a cup of tea and a view of the river?"

If only the river would reveal to her his God.

Chapter 6

Julia approached the boathouse where William stood with paintbrush in hand. "I'm ready to help again today."

The boathouse, weathered by long Northern New York winters and winds, needed a fresh coat, a rejuvenating touch to withstand another year of harsh river life. They'd been working at it for two days and had made good progress, but her muscles ached from the unaccustomed exercise.

William raised an eyebrow, a bemused smile playing on his lips. "A change of wardrobe, Gingersnap?"

She chuckled nervously, tickled by hearing the affectionate moniker. It brought warm memories of her father calling her that as she adjusted the sash over her shirtwaist. "Well, your mother thought these might be more suitable for the task at hand, especially after I splattered paint on my skirt yesterday."

The woolen trousers, though loose on her frame, provided freedom of movement she hadn't experienced in the restrictive layers of her skirts. She blushed, feeling a little exposed as the unfamiliar fabric brushed against her legs. "She insisted I wear them, though I hope I don't damage them in the process."

William's laughter echoed along the shore. "I'm sure Mother is delighted to see her trousers put to good use. She only wears them in the winter, and even if you damaged them, she's an expert seamstress and could make another pair in no time. Now, let's get to work on the rest of this boathouse. The privy shed shouldn't take more than an hour, so I think we can finish everything today."

Julia took the brush he offered, dipped it in the paint, and made long, sweeping strokes. "I never thought I'd be doing manual labor like this, but I'm actually enjoying it. There's something rewarding about working on such a large and unfamiliar canvas. It certainly is a novel experience for me."

William grinned at her eagerness. "Well, that's the spirit. We make a good team. The fancy city life didn't afford you such luxuries?"

She shook her head, glancing down at her legs. "Never. And folks in the city would frown upon me wearing Aunt Dee's trousers."

He chuckled. "Their loss."

In between strokes of paint, Julia stole glances at William, who seemed more amused than surprised by her unconventional attire. The cool, sunlit morning turned into a melody of shared laughter accented by the swish of brushes against the boathouse walls. The waves crashed against the rocky shore, their measured sound a backdrop to their work and conversation.

As they worked side by side, Julia embraced the wide-legged garment that allowed her to move freely. She climbed the ladder and reached corners with ease. The trousers permitted a sense of empowerment, liberating her from the constraints of convention.

When William dipped his brush the same time as she, he stopped and glanced at her, his blue eyes divulging a hint of melancholy. "I've never really talked about my father, have I? Has my mother told you the tale of his passing?"

Julia shook her head, welcoming him to share the sad chapter of his family's life. "No, and I was afraid to ask. I was unsure of resurrecting pain."

"Captain William Dodge, my father, was a remarkable man." His tone, so loving and respectful, reminded her of how she felt about her own father. "He was the first lighthouse keeper here, you know. A stalwart guardian of the river, guiding ships through stormy nights. Everything I know about tending this place is because of him."

"Then he must have been a great man."

Her tone echoed his, surprising her with how her growing affection for him slipped from her lips.

"But before he became keeper, before I was born, he was a captain—a hero in the Civil War." A hint of nostalgia crept into his voice as he spoke of his role model. "He fought with the New York volunteers, but not without his share of scars. His left foot was badly wounded in battle, so he limped the rest of his life."

William's gaze wandered to the lighthouse, as if searching the distant horizon for the memories of his father's past. "In 1870, following his appointment as the first keeper of Sister Island Lighthouse, he served faithfully and cheerfully. For twenty-three years, he tended to this tower, the keeper of both the light and its stories."

Julia nodded, affirming his pride in his father. "Was he here during the explosion you told me about?"

His brow rose. "We all were. I was seven, and it was terrifying."

"Of course." She rolled her eyes. Arithmetic never was her forte.

A wistful smile graced his face as he continued. "Before the lighthouse, he was a man of many trades—a cabinetmaker, a tax collector, a census enumerator. A life woven with diverse endeavors, each one contributing to the rich testimony of his existence."

She listened, captivated by the tale of a man who had worn so many different hats throughout his life. "That's quite a menagerie of jobs."

William's eyes glinted with affection. "True. My father wasn't just a keeper of the light. He was a craftsman too. He made that sideboard in the parlor. Every time I look at it, I see not just a piece of furniture but a legacy of his craftsmanship."

"I know the one. It's beautiful."

Julia's heart warmed. The revelation of even this small aspect of his father forged a tender kinship. Aunt Dee's husband. How deeply she must feel his loss.

The sound of a ship's passing filled the momentary lull between them.

"He passed away last year, from dropsy of the heart." William's tone spoke of both reverence and respect. "But he taught me well, so his legacy lives on—not just in that lighthouse, but in the stories, the sideboard, and in me."

Julia reached for his hand, offering comfort. "Thank you for sharing this with me, William. I'm sorry for your loss. I wish I'd known him."

They fell into a peaceful silence as they worked, brushes in hand, transforming the weathered shed and boathouse into refurbished structures that complemented the loveliness of the surrounding nature. The steady swipe of bristles against wood resumed, providing a comforting cadence, and the pungent scent of fresh paint filled the air.

"So, Julia," he began, breaking the companionable quiet that had settled between them. "Tell me more about Walden Pond. I confess, I haven't read the book."

She dipped her brush into the paint, contemplating his question. "It's more than just a pond. For Thoreau, it became his sacred sanctuary. A place where he found peace, away from the expectations and judgments of the world."

He nodded. "I'm glad his time there helped him. But I'm curious about something else. How can someone, surrounded by nature, not believe in something greater?"

Her grip tightened on the brush. The question dangled between them like an unspoken challenge. "As I've said before, like Thoreau, I find my connection to the universe in the simplicity of nature, and in the science that explains it all, as did my father. I don't need a divine entity to find meaning and purpose."

"But isn't there a sense of astonishment, a spiritual communion, in acknowledging the Creator?" He furrowed his brow, a hint of disagreement creeping into his voice. "That Someone who designed this intricate tapestry we call life?"

She sighed, setting down her paintbrush. "The awe-inspiring beauty of the natural world and the power of human intellect is enough for me. I don't need to attribute it to a higher power. This river, the trees, the animals—they are all part of a delicate, self-sustaining balance that doesn't require divine intervention."

He shook his head, a subtle frustration clouding his features. "I cannot fathom a world without purpose, without a Creator guiding us. Moreover, the Bible reveals His *scientific* design. Only humans show an awareness of God, sin, morality, and life beyond death, as the book explains. Only humans demonstrate advancement in civilization, agriculture, and technology, as the stories of the Bible describe. And the Bible shares lots of scientific realities, from the earth being round to the origin of life to astronomy—even to the disappearing dinosaurs. I find science in so many pages of the Creator's book. Relying only on creation for the answers seems so . . . empty."

"Empty? No, William, it's liberating. It means we have the responsibility and the freedom to shape our own destinies, to find meaning in our actions and connections. We're not bound by the limitations of dogma or the whims of some distant deity."

Their conversation had shifted from the tranquility of working together to the intensity of conflicting beliefs. Again. And she was tired of it. The air between them crackled with tension, each stroke of the brush like a declaration of their contrasting perspectives. For several minutes, neither spoke. The sounds of nature around intensified, as if reciting the internal struggles she faced.

Would their differences drive a wedge between them, or was there, perhaps, a way to bridge the gap and appreciate nature in their individual worldviews? If she was truthful, their conversations and William's peace-filled faith challenged her to question her beliefs more each day.

Did she really believe all that she touted, or was she simply clinging to her father's views to keep him close? Perhaps, if she were honest, it might also be a smidgen of the rebellion that had ruled her life from the time she was little. Mother had been so adamant about her religious convictions, belittling her father, even laughing at him. She had watched her parents fight over faith and wanted nothing to do with it. The memories still hurt.

Yet William and Aunt Dee's unwavering faith reminded her of the calm river before her and stood as firm as the bedrock beneath her feet. Despite her mother and these admirable folks sharing a testimony of the same God, the faith on this island bore a distinctly authentic quality.

But was it truly sincere?

William stood with Julia and admired their completed work. A sense of accomplishment enveloped him as the boathouse stood resplendent in its fresh coat as the sun dappled the scene.

"Thank you for the help, Julia. That was one big job I had wanted to finish before the lighthouse inspector, Lieutenant Worthington, pays a call. It would have taken me three times as long without you." A teasing grin spread across his face. "And those trousers seemed to speed you along. I'll have to thank Mother too."

Julia giggled, a potpourri of relief and satisfaction in her eyes. "Who knew trousers could be so liberating and that hard work could be so much fun?" She pointed to a skiff in the distance where three young teens cavorted. "Those girls remind me too much of me in my younger days. Silly. Self-centered. A little reckless."

He responded with a dip of his chin as laughter skipped across the water, the playful antics of the girls visible even from afar. The hair on the back of his neck prickled, standing at attention as it always did when danger was present.

As the skiff rocked perilously, the girls' unfettered merriment turned to panic.

Julia gasped. "They've tipped the boat over!"

Without a second thought, he sprang into action. To his surprise, Julia did, too, beating him to the skiff. Her face bore the same intensity as he felt.

The tumult of the rescue electrified the air as they launched the boat. The oars sliced through the water with a determined cadence. The urgency of the situation propelled them forward.

As they approached the distressed girls, now soaked and clinging to the sides of the boat, the three greeted them with a combination of relief and embarrassment. The playful atmosphere had shifted to a sober acknowledgment of the river's power.

"Grab on, girls!" His command echoed on the water as Julia extended a steady hand to the shivering teenagers. With a mixture of nervous laughter and gratitude, they clambered into the skiff, their sodden clothes sticking to their skin.

The girl who appeared to be the leader of the pack cleared her throat. "We live on Grenadier."

William glanced at the nearby island. "You're from the farms?"

All three nodded.

He turned the rowboat toward the safety of the Grenadier Island shore.

Julia, her eyes gleaming with a blend of amusement and camaraderie, chuckled at the escapade. "A bit of excitement for the day, aye?"

The girls, still catching their breath, exchanged sheepish glances. "We thought we could handle it," one of them admitted, a blush tinting her cheeks.

After dropping them safely onto the island, he bid them farewell, flashing a reassuring smile. "The river always keeps us on our toes, doesn't it? Be sure to retrieve the boat before nightfall, or it won't be there tomorrow morning."

The girls' eyes widened, as if they hadn't considered being found out. They would have some explaining to do. And soon.

A gentle sparkle lit Julia's eyes as they rowed back to Sister. "Upon my arrival here, I envisioned this island as a mundane, solitary confinement. Yet there's a thrilling aspect of it absent in the city. I admit, I've developed a fondness for the unconventional—be it in my attire, in rescuing rebellious girls, or simply in painting a boathouse . . . and residing at a lighthouse."

"I'm delighted to know that, Gingersnap. As for me, it's time to put my love for the job to use and light that lamp. Come with me to the lamp room, and I'll treat you to a sunset that's absolutely breathtaking."

When they got back to Sister Island, the sun had begun its slow journey to the horizon, splashing the water with pink, orange, and red. He took hold of her hand, playfully tugging her toward the cottage, relishing the evening's unfolding events and strengthening the camaraderie between them. Thankfully, they found his mother peacefully asleep in her chair. At least for now, he had Julia all to himself.

Once they reached the lamp room, he quickly lit the lamp, the sweet sound of laughter lingering in the evening air. As the sunset began its marvelous performance, it cast a brilliant display of colors across the sky, just as he had hoped, and the radiant glow took their breath away. Dramatic shadows added depth to the scene.

He gestured toward the expanse of the St. Lawrence River with a deep appreciation for the subtle intricacies that decorated the river.

Perhaps, if he could help her grasp his profound appreciation of the Creator's amazing work, she might turn her eyes to Him. Then, they could find common ground in what was really important. "What captures my attention in this moment is the exquisite textures of the choppy water."

Julia nodded, rolling her hands around each other. "It's like a living masterpiece, different from the other days when the waves flow by in smoother rhythms."

The afterglow of sunset created a captivating mosaic of light and shadow before them. He marveled at its beauty. "It's as if the river is playing with the sun."

Julia waved an arm wide across the view. "And this is why I want to paint a sunset. Perhaps tomorrow."

He jerked his head in her direction. "Do it! Look for texture—it's everywhere, from the weathered grain of a fallen tree trunk to the delicate water droplets clinging to a window after a passing rain. Textures add that extra layer of visual interest, an invitation to delve deeper into the intricate details that often go unnoticed. And in it, I find a kind of poetry—a language spoken only by the land, the water, and the air."

Julia's brow furrowed as she contemplated it, but then she agreed. "I hadn't thought of it that way, though I strive to give my work a distinctiveness you want to touch. Yet your sentiments have given me much to think about. Thank you."

He was breaking through, wasn't he? "Of course. I believe that texture can be a storyteller, and I long to capture its intricacies whenever I paint."

"Maybe we could work side by side?" She nibbled on her lip, scanning his face with hopeful anticipation.

He shrugged. If only . . . "Perhaps, though nighttime is when I work, and I'm not as gifted as you are. I create purely for the fun of it, but your art . . . your work has a way of bringing a scene to life."

"Julia? Are you up there?" Mother's voice drifted up the tower and held a hint of concern. "William, is she there?"

He tossed Julia a wink. "Yes, Mother, she's safe and sound. We didn't want to disturb your nap."

Julia bid him goodnight and scurried down the ladder. "I'm fine, Aunt Dee. Coming. Just enjoying the sunset from up here."

As she departed, a profound sense of emptiness engulfed him. Even though they challenged each other, the preceding three days had grown a garden of sweet kinship, a closeness previously unfelt. It surpassed the bonds he had with his father, his mother, or even Louise.

Yet beneath it all loomed the stark reality—she still didn't embrace what held the utmost importance to him—his faith.

William grappled with the incomprehensible absence of it in her life. The unwavering depth of his belief in the Triune God and a personal relationship with the Savior stood as the cornerstone of his existence. It wasn't just a part of his life—it lent strength to his spirit and upheld him in times of need.

So, the question gnawed at him most of the night—how could she elevate creation above the Creator who orchestrated it all? Even the thought of engaging his heart with this captivating woman involved an enticing but dangerous dance, and he feared that, in turning toward her, he might inadvertently turn away from God.

Chapter 7

Inspired by the tranquility of the moment and determined to depict the lighthouse at sunset, Julia gathered her art supplies and made her way to an eastern spot on the island. From here, she could capture the lighthouse and the western sunset. The early-evening sun kissed the shores of Sister Island, radiating on the landscape. A symphony of bird calls, lapping waves, and buzzing insects filled the air, a familiar melody to accompany and inspire her artistic endeavors.

The river breeze carried whispers of tales untold as Julia dipped her brush into the palette, her heart beating to the ebb and flow of the breakers crashing against the rocky shore. The lighthouse held secrets etched into its weathered exterior, bathed in shades of the slowly setting sun, and she would do her best to capture each one.

Julia's hands trembled with anticipation and reverence as she sketched the silhouette of Sister Island Lighthouse. The canvas lay before her like a blank chapter waiting to be written. Each stroke was like a waltz between the brush and the page, a hushed conversation with the lighthouse she'd come to love.

When did that happen? She wasn't sure, but she'd contemplate that later.

The sky, now ablaze with the fiery farewell of the sun, embodied her growing feelings about its lightkeeper. The small flame he'd sparked in her was quickly becoming a burning fire, prompting her to reevaluate everything in her life.

Beautiful, but scary too.

William emerged from the cottage and made his way toward her, but she stayed deeply engrossed in capturing the enchanting sight of the setting sun spilling its luxurious beams on the river and lighthouse before the light faded. Lost in the moment, she barely acknowledged his presence.

"Good evening, Gingersnap." William's voice carried a touch of regret. "Sorry I can't join you, but duty calls, you know. Perhaps we can create side by side under the bright light of day."

Julia smiled, confirming his words with a nod but maintaining her dedication to the painting. "I understand, William. Truly."

"May I take a peek, please?"

"Certainly." She paused her brushstrokes. "Though I fear I'll struggle to capture the splendor of this evening before the light bids its farewell."

William slipped quietly behind her, then gasped as he took in her work in progress. "Texture galore. I can almost feel the waves and the setting sun. Glorious, Julia. Just glorious!"

In his enthusiasm, he touched her shoulder, his proximity emphasizing their shared appreciation for the art unfolding before them. His breath tickled her ear as he leaned closer and whispered, "Don't stop. Don't ever stop."

With those words, he swiftly retreated to the cottage, leaving her quivering from his accolades. Minutes later, light exploded across the water, scattering an ethereal glow on the river and affirming the magic of that fleeting moment.

She lost herself in the process, each brushstroke a meditation on the grandeur that surrounded her. Her senses came alive as the wind carried the musky scent of the river, and the distant call of seagulls added their serenade.

Julia scrambled to capture the essence of Sister Island—the way twilight played upon the weathered stones, the delicate waltz of seagulls in the air, and the quiet strength that emanated from the lighthouse itself. She captured her connection to the lighthouse in an unexpected moment that brought tears to her eyes.

Once this summer was gone . . . she'd never be the same.

When the first stars emerged in the darkening sky, Julia's strokes became more fervent. The waves, once a chant of crashing crescendos, now whispered haunting lullabies. A lone seagull soared above, a fleeting silhouette against the beauty of twilight. As she watched it, she sighed a plea for freedom, for release from the weight of unanswered questions that bombarded her.

The lighthouse, its light now casting long shadows, stood tall as a sentry over her murky struggle. She was falling head over heels for the man in the tower who lived a solitary life under the call of a higher being she didn't understand.

Would she ever fathom what made him tick?

Her last stroke fell like an exhale, and Julia stepped back, her chest rising and falling with the sound of the lapping waves. The image before her was more than pigment on canvas—it emulated the battles fought within, a visual symphony of her confusing emotions.

As darkness embraced the world, Julia packed her tools, leaving the light to keep its solitary vigil. And as she walked away, the night whispered promises of a new dawn, where the colors of the sunrise would paint hope on the horizon.

The pleasant flicker from the oil lamp beckoned Julia to join Aunt Dee on the kitchen porch. Fireflies flitted all around her, sparking joy amid Julia's trials. With a wide grin, the older woman patted the seat of the worn wooden chair next to her. "Come, dearie, and enjoy this lovely evening with me."

Julia set her work and supplies inside on the kitchen table and returned to the porch where Aunt Dee sat, her head tilted and brows questioning. "I'd show you, but it isn't quite finished. I'd like to complete it first, if you don't mind."

The older woman grasped her hand. "Of course,

dearie. I've been watching you work from here, and even from this distance, you exuded an intensity and thoughtfulness that mesmerized me. When William told me how fabulous your work was, I knew you were in your artistic frenzy."

Julia giggled. "I don't know about that, but I do get absorbed in the process, I must admit. And tonight's sunset was amazing."

"It certainly was." Aunt Dee pointed south. "I was just wondering why the Revenue Marine Service boat is passing by tonight. It's an unusual time for them."

"The what?"

Aunt Dee jerked her chin toward a boat brightly lit and labeled, *Revenue Marine Service*. "There, by Third Brother Island. Do you know about them?"

She shook her head. "Nothing, especially since I'm Canadian. I can guess they're involved in maritime activities, but that's about it."

Aunt Dee leaned back and chuckled, her hands folded in her lap. "Of course. Well, my dear, it has a rich history, one that stretches back to the founding of our nation. It was established in 1790 by none other than Secretary of the Treasury Alexander Hamilton."

Julia furrowed her brows. "It sure has a strange name."

"Indeed." Aunt Dee tilted her head, a hint of nostalgia in her voice. "The government is now talking about renaming it the United States Coast Guard, but Congress can't make up its mind. It was initially tasked with enforcing tariffs and trade laws, but they also collected revenue to fund our fledgling nation. Thus, the name. It's the oldest continuous seagoing service in the United States, even older than our navy, and it has been a stalwart presence since the Constitution became the law of the land in 1789."

Julia leaned in. "Interesting." Her friend and mentor was a wealth of information—and wisdom, that was certain.

Aunt Dee smiled, her eyes radiating deep appreciation. "Their job is to safeguard our shores during times of war, conduct search and rescue missions, ensure maritime safety, and even protect the river. It's a jack-of-all-trades on the water, dedicated to serving and protecting."

"I don't know that Canada has anything like that. Do they protect all of the river, even when the Canadian waters bleed into America's?"

Aunt Dee's eyes fixed on the horizon. "I'm sure they do. It doesn't matter which country needs help. They just serve those in need. Like my husband did, and now my son does."

A sense of admiration for river life enveloped Julia, stirring within her a deep appreciation for the complexities it held. To her surprise and, per-haps, chagrin, the remote expanse of this island, shared only with Aunt Dee and her son, had made its way into her affections. And amidst the stillness, William, the keeper of the light, was assuredly securing a place in her heart too.

William stood on the lighthouse parapet as he scanned the dark night. Long after midnight, a menacing fog crept in and clung to the waters of the St. Lawrence, shrouding the river in danger. His pulse quickened as he scanned the murky river, but the heavy mist reduced his visibility to nothing.

A ship sounded, and then another as William attempted to follow the haunting distress calls through the cloudy gloom. Again, they sounded, and the hair on the back of his neck prickled with alarm.

Where were the two ships? If they couldn't see the light through the fog, surely, disaster could unfold beneath its veil.

A deafening collision reverberated through the night, and his heart raced with fear and urgency. Gripping the parapet railing, he strained to peer through the thick fog, desperate to glimpse the doomed vessels. They had to be near . . . too near.

His nerves fired as the haunting sound of metal against metal screeched a cacophony of destruction in the darkness. His mind raced, knowing there were lives hanging in the balance below, unseen and at the mercy of the fog. He cursed the treacherous weather that masked the scene from his vigilant gaze.

As the ominous scraping persisted, a chilling realization set him in motion—he was the only beacon of hope for these people in peril. The responsibility weighed heavily on his shoulders, but every second counted. He slid down the ladder of the lighthouse, his lantern in hand.

Julia met him at the bottom of the ladder, shaking like a leaf in the wind, her eyes wide with fear. "What was that?"

He had no time for chatter. "A collision! Quick. I'll need your help. Mother's too."

Julia pressed her lips together and nodded, fleeing to her room. Hopefully, she would relay the matter to his mother. As he scurried down the stairs and ran toward danger, he prayed the two women would quickly join him to help.

He followed the wails and shouts of sailors in need as the beam of light weakly cut through the fog, exposing fragments of wreckage strewn across the water. A steamer and a barge, now entangled in a dervish of destruction, groaned under the strain of their collision. His heart sank as he frantically scanned the debris for survivors.

The wails of the wounded pierced the darkness, mixing with the terrible sound of metal against metal. The heavy mist chilled his face as he strained to assess the situation through the fog.

A lone sailor trudged out of the water and

scanned William's keeper's uniform. His face held terror. "I'm first mate of the Canadian passenger-and-freight steamer *Ocean*. Captain says the American barge *Kent* had no lights. In this pea soup, we hit the shoal, and the barge hit us!" The man thrust splayed fingers in front of William's face. "The *Kent* was the last in a string of five barges being towed downriver by the tug *Seymour*, which was heavily laden with coal. Both our *Ocean* and the *Kent* are now sinking, and two of our deckhands, who were asleep on the *Ocean*'s aft deck, are feared drowned."

William clasped the sailor's arm. "Are there many others in danger, sir?"

The man shook his head, droplets of water flying through the air. "We were sailing with a small crew, sir, and no passengers, thank God. Most of the sailors have jumped ship and are congregating over yonder." He pointed to the far end of the island before leaving William's side, still relaying information as he fled. "A few are still in the water, and several are injured. Don't know about the *Kent* crew."

Within moments, Julia and Mother joined him. "Thank God you're here. Mother, will you please telegraph for help?" He filled her in on the details he'd learned from the first mate.

Mother patted his arm. "I'll call for help."

"What can I do?" Julia wrung her hands, shifting her weight from one foot to the other.

William touched her shoulder, hoping to calm her. "Go with Mother and get the medical supplies and as much cloth for bandages as you can. Blankets, too, if you can carry them. She'll show you where to find them."

Julia hurried off, disappearing into the murky fog within yards of him. The fate of those on the ships rested on his shoulders, so he raised his lantern high against the fog that still concealed most of the lighthouse beam as he rushed to the riverbank.

His heart pounded, and the acrid scent of burning coal accosted his nose. The cries of those still in the water pierced the eerie sounds of the pieces of wreckage bumping against each other. A few more sailors swam to shore or floated in on bits of the ships before collapsing on the shore and then joining their mates.

Julia returned with a large basket laden with supplies and set it on the ground. "Your mother has called for assistance, and I'm here to help."

A young sailor, bleeding from his head, hobbled up to them and picked up the basket. "I can't swim, but I know first aid. I'll tend to the injured. Please go and save who you can!"

Julia grabbed the lantern from William, its feeble rays barely piercing the dense fog. She followed him to the water's edge, and plunged in knee deep.

Amidst the debris, William spotted a small row-boat apparently from one of the vessels floating among the remnants of the *Ocean* and the *Kent*. Both vessels were now being swallowed by the unforgiving depths, sinking quickly into the murky darkness.

Julia gripped William's forearm with one hand and pointed to a flailing man in the river with the other. "We need to help the survivors still in danger."

William nodded, and together they jumped into the abandoned rowboat. Why no one had commandeered it before now was a mystery.

As he rowed toward the collision site, the lantern's light shone across the water, dimly illuminating a few desperate faces of those clinging to bits of wreckage, their cries for help barely audible above the commotion.

Closer to the wreck, Julia's eyes widened. "Oh no!" Two men in uniform lay face down and lifeless in the cold embrace of the river. "They're already dead, William. Shall I pull them in?"

He shook his head. "We can't save them, Julia, but we can help the others."

With renewed determination, he and Julia focused on the living, pulling three survivors into the rowboat. When their tiny boat was heavy laden, an officer on the *Seymour* took charge and coordinated the water rescue efforts just as the Revenue Marine Service arrived.

William returned to the island with the survivors. Julia helped the injured out of the boat.

While he made a bonfire to ward off the chill, she bandaged a burn on one sailor and cleaned and bound the wound of another.

The burned man's gratitude overflowed. "Thank you, miss. If you hadn't come, I wouldn't have made it."

Once the fire was blazing and men had gathered around to warm themselves, William helped Julia by placing a splint on a possibly fractured ankle while she wrapped strips of cloth around the man's leg to secure it. That done, she offered words of comfort to the shaken survivors and helped lead the land efforts with calm authority. Nearby, Mother also aided those in need. He was truly blessed to have these compassionate women here to help.

The three of them worked through the night tending the men, keeping the fire going, and offering hot coffee. Mother kept the drink brewing and managed the folks who came to help. As was the custom, neighbors heard the call for help and arrived from both the American mainland and the nearby Canadian island of Grenadier, taking two or three men at a time to care for until only a handful of men remained.

The Revenue Marine Service assessed the situation, interviewed those they could, and aided where necessary. Their near proximity on such a night was nothing short of providential.

As the first light of dawn broke through the

dissipating fog, the last of the rescue boats loaded the final four sailors and returned to their homes with their charges.

Mother waved as they departed. "You'll be in our prayers, men."

William added, "And thanks for your help, neighbors."

Julia stood with them until the boat disappeared into the mist. She wiped her brow with her shirtsleeve. "Whew! I'm exhausted. That was a long, scary night, but it felt good to do a good deed. I never had a chance to do anything like that in the city."

William nodded, his body aching with the weariness too. "It's what we do here at the lighthouse. We serve as God's hands and feet helping others."

Julia's brow furrowed deep, and a cynical chuckle escaped her lips. "God's hands and feet? Really?"

Mother nodded. "Really, dearie. I'm tired too, so I'm going to bed, you two."

After she left, an unpleasant awareness swept over William. He stood next to Julia, united by circumstance but divided by ideology, as the lighthouse beam swept over them, lobbing alternating shadows across her perplexed face.

The collision between the ships had brought them together, but it also illuminated the fault lines in their camaraderie, just when he was beginning to hope for more. The unity they'd found in the face of disaster couldn't bridge the gap that existed in their souls.

Perhaps nothing ever would.

Chapter 8

The sound of raindrops against the window created a soothing background as Julia sat by the fireplace, the constant flickering of the flames illuminating the pages of the Bible in her hands. The smell of damp earth lingered in the air, a reminder of the three-day storm that had kept them indoors after the wreck.

Once she'd finished her sunset painting, she had turned her attention to deeper matters—those of the heart. After that fateful night rescuing others, the idea of exploring the Bible had crossed her mind. Something was different about her companions, and she was determined to find out what.

As Aunt Dee had suggested, Julia delved into the Psalms and New Testament and was captivated by the teachings and stories within their pages. The words came alive, resonating with a depth that touched her soul. The characters she met and the lessons she read fascinated her, stirring a longing to understand the source of the unwavering faith, the joy and peace, that influenced William and his mother.

But separating her own mother's religious hypocrisy and this book was no easy task. Her mother had spewed Scripture, used it as a weapon against her father and herself. How could she reconcile that?

Julia looked up from her reading at William and his mother. Maybe they could help?

Aunt Dee sat across from her tatting a white collar and matching cuffs. She looked up and smiled. "How are you finding it, dearie?" The woman's eyes reflected genuine curiosity. "Any questions?"

"Too many to voice just yet." She flipped a page. "It's . . . different. I mean, in a good way. There's a sort of peace in these words. They bring clarity to things that I've wanted to know."

Aunt Dee nodded. "That book has a unique way of touching hearts, and it is a great source of wisdom and comfort for many."

For those three days, Julia did little else but explore the Scriptures, sometimes with Aunt Dee by her side, at other times engaging in challenging discussions with William. The cozy parlor became a cocoon for exploration, curiosity, and the pursuit of something deeper than everyday life. And in that journey, she felt safe.

In contrast to her mother's rigid adherence to a dogmatic religion of strict rules and the looming threat of consequences, William and Aunt Dee extended an abundance of grace and mercy. They embraced her patiently and compassionately, accepting her exactly as she was.

On the third stormy afternoon, as the showers

persisted outside, she sat with William near the fireplace. The flames swayed, flickering shadows on the walls as she posed a question that had been lingering in her mind. "Why does your faith bring you so much hope and peace?"

He leaned back as if contemplating her query. "It's about love, really. The love we find in God, the love He has for us, and the love we share with others. It's a source of strength, a compass that guides me even in the toughest times."

As he spoke, hope enveloped her, a sense of connection to something beyond the material world. The rain continued to tap against the windows, but inside, a different kind of storm was brewing—a storm of introspection and even deeper discovery Julia couldn't ignore.

As she continued to absorb the warmth emanating from the fireplace, her mind became a battleground of conflicting thoughts and emotions. Would embracing the faith that surrounded her mean abandoning the principles her father had instilled in her? What of her father's philosphy of self-reliance and his adoration of nature— the belief that strength came from within and that the natural world held all the answers? Was it an empty fallacy? Would turning toward a different path, a path of faith, be a betrayal of everything he had taught her? And the rejection of the sturdy foundation of independence he had worked so hard to build within her, treachery?

Would choosing another way of life be a Judas kiss?

Her uncertainties deepened as she contemplated the idea of surrendering to a distant power, a force that would forevermore order her steps. The God her mother had known, the one *she* had rejected, seemed ineffective. If that deity truly dictated the path of her mother's life, then why did it lead to ridicule, neglect, and the prioritization of social expectations over familial bonds? That was certainly not the God Julia experienced here.

Her thoughts circled back to her father, who, for all his strength and love, lacked the peace that radiated from William and his mother. Father's convictions often led to spasmodic agitation and a frantic, fervent need to validate his beliefs, even if it meant shunning those who questioned him. But was that aggressive stance the only way to stand firm in one's convictions—as she had been doing?

The storm of introspection raged within, but she couldn't deny the allure of what she saw here on the island. The faith the Dodges offered transcended the struggles of daily life. Instead, like a magnet, it pulled her toward something unfamiliar yet undeniably appealing.

Still, she had to know more.

The late-spring showers persisted outside, a steady cadence that echoed the drumming of her heartbeat. According to William, the book in her hands held the answers to all the questions she hadn't dared to ask before now. So a decision weighed heavy on her shoulders—whether to cling to the familiar shores of her father's beliefs or venture into the uncharted waters of William's and his mother's faith.

When he stood and excused himself, Julia looked up from her introspection. He left the room and returned holding a kazoo, an amusing glint in his eye. A wide grin adorned his face, exposing a set of straight white teeth that added a touch of charm to his handsome countenance.

Julia raised an eyebrow but giggled with delight. "Another concert, William?" She closed the book, ready for a lighthearted diversion.

Aunt Dee shrugged, a chuckle escaping her lips. Her gaze darted from her son to Julia. "Wait till you hear it, dearie. It's jolly fun."

With no introduction, William put the kazoo to his lips and began playing the familiar strains of "Oh My Darling, Clementine."

Julia burst into laughter. The kazoo's comical tones turned the classic tune into a whimsical rendition.

Not missing a beat, William transitioned seamlessly to "Rock-a-bye Baby." Julia swayed with it as if cradling an imaginary baby, a grin plastered on her face.

The kazoo's buzzing sound took on a new life as William launched into "Polly Wolly Doodle."

He tapped his toe as he played, and lighthearted joy filled the room. He must have sensed she needed this reprieve.

She and Aunt Dee clapped along, thoroughly entertained by the unexpected concert. Laughter filled the room, the quirky tunes turning a somber afternoon into a lively and memorable performance. A sweet relief from deep ponderings and the gloom of stormy days.

When he was done, William took a bow, the kazoo still in hand.

They applauded enthusiastically, and Julia cheered. "Bravo! I've never heard a kazoo before nor knew it could be so entertaining."

William took a seat on the settee next to his mother. He winked, a grin playing on his lips. The mischievous glimmer in his eyes piqued Julia's curiosity. He looked as though he had other surprises in store for them.

"William, what's got you looking like the cat that ate the canary?"

He chuckled, leaning in. "Have you ever heard the history of the kazoo, my little gingersnap?"

"The kazoo? I've never even heard one played until now."

William held up the tin instrument. "About fifty years ago, in Macon, Georgia, a man named Alabama Vest wanted a simple instrument to play, so he asked a German clockmaker to make it for him."

Her curiosity deepened. "A German clockmaker made a musical instrument?"

Aunt Dee nodded, confirming her son's tale. Apparently, she knew the story too.

William smiled. "Exactly. Alabama Vest knew what he wanted, and Thaddeus Von Clegg was the man for the job. So this odd duo birthed the kazoo. As you now see, the kazoo has a cheerful charm, a simplicity that resonates with people."

She smiled at William's animated storytelling.

Aunt Dee quirked her eyebrows. "Why did you call Julia 'Gingersnap,' son?"

William guffawed. "Just look at that hair and those beautiful eyes. That's why."

Aunt Dee frowned, flinging a concerned glance at Julia. "Are you okay with that, dearie?"

Julia nodded, a spirited chuckle escaping her lips. "Of course. That was my father's pet name for me, and it brings comforting memories to my heart."

Aunt Dee blew out a breath. "Well, all right, then. Gingersnap it is."

William bowed playfully. "And now, if you'll excuse me, I must go and attend the light. I hope you enjoyed a bit of music and some history to boot. Goodnight, Mother. Gingersnap."

"Goodnight, William. And thank you."

William winked at her, pecked his mother on the cheek, and disappeared into the shadows. Julia smiled at the camaraderie and the lighthearted nickname. The moment lingered, leaving behind harmony and acceptance that made her feel right at home.

But the Bible on her lap once again sparked her attention. How long could she put off settling those deeper matters?

William ascended the staircase, the familiar creaks of the lighthouse stairs resounding in the quiet space. He climbed the ladder and reached the lamp room, his sanctuary where the beacon that guided sailors through the night awaited his care.

He sighed as he set the kazoo on the lamp room bench. He patted it gently, a wordless expression of gratitude for the simple delight it had brought to the women in the parlor. His mother and Julia seemed pleased, and that gave him a small sense of accomplishment.

He'd felt Julia needed it. The way she had delved into his parents' Bible for the past few days, emotions playing across her face like shadows cast by a flickering flame, had unsettled him. Joy, fear, sorrow, confusion—each expression etched into his memory. Yet he resisted the urge to pry, to bombard her with questions about what she was discovering within those well-worn pages.

But her introspective gloom weighed heavily on his mind. Since she hadn't wanted to be here in the first place, perhaps she might want to leave Sister Island to escape the isolation and monotony. Three days cooped up in the cottage had a way of amplifying the island's solitude. He understood the desire for a sabbatical to the mainland, and on days like these, he yearned for a change of scenery too.

He couldn't imagine her absence. Hated the thought of life without her.

Yet he had a nagging feeling that her troubled spirit ran deeper than mere island weariness. His concern for her wasn't solely about the weathered walls of the lighthouse or the persistent sound of crashing waves or even the deluge over the past few days. It was a concern born from sensing she was on a life-altering spiritual journey—and the growing feelings he had for her.

As William scanned the lamp room, it smelled of dampness and kerosene, scents ingrained in the very fabric of the lighthouse. The rain continued to patter incessantly on the ten-sided glass room, a staccato call to be at attention, though he doubted many would traverse the river in such weather, save the oceangoing salties or perhaps a laker or two already en route to port. Still, after the recent crash, he felt the need to remain vigilant.

He approached the massive lamp, that giant sentinel in the center of the room, and lit it. The wick flickered, a dim flame yearning for attention. He sighed. Much like the lamp, there were aspects of his heart that also needed tending.

He carefully fine-tuned the wick, coaxing it to life with a gentle adjustment. The flame responded, dancing with renewed vigor.

William polished the brass components of the lamp until they gleamed, each stroke a subtle swish of reflection. The windows of the lamp room also caught his attention. With a determined resolve, he set about cleaning them, but the view beyond the glass was obscured, much like the uncertainty that clouded his tomorrows.

As he wiped away the residue, he appraised Julia's inner storm and the book that held the answers to her battle. Though she hadn't mentioned the many notes and comments his father and mother had added to their family heirloom, he knew many of them by heart. Indeed, he had added a few of his own over the years.

He wouldn't force Julia to share her revelations. No, he had to let her come to him when she was ready. In the meantime, he would pray for her.

He set about puttering, as he often did when deep in thought. The clang of metal against metal resounded through the lamp room as he tinkered with the brass workings of the massive apparatus. He smiled as the beam of light from the lighthouse swept across the stormy river, cutting through the thick mist that clung to the island and beyond, just as it should.

Footfalls on the ladder sounded at the hatch door. A feminine hand, the wrist adorned with a silver bracelet, plunked a steaming mug of something onto the floor. Julia's head and shoulders emerged, a smile on her face, as she set another mug next to the first one.

His heart skipped several beats at the sight of her. "Well, if it isn't my favorite gingersnap. What brings you up here on a night like this?"

Julia laughed, her eyes sparkling. "I made some hot cocoa. Your mother thought you'd enjoy a cup. It feels more like early spring than the middle of June, doesn't it?"

He grinned, wiping his hands on a cloth before reaching for her hand and tugging her up to the platform. Then he grasped both mugs, handed one to her, and clinked his to hers. "Thank you and cheers! You seem to know how to revive my heart, even on the chilliest nights." He took a sip, savoring the rich chocolatey comfort. "Ah, this is perfect. How did I get so lucky to have you and my mother conspiring to spoil me?"

She winked, her gaze wandering to the stormy riverscape beyond the lighthouse windows. "It's a thank you for the concert, which dispelled the rainy-day gloom quite nicely. Your mother has retired for the evening, so I thought I'd chat with you for a while."

As the showers drummed against the windows, he took another sip. "I'm glad, Gingersnap. I'd hoped you'd pay me a visit before heading to bed. These stormy days . . ." He glanced out at the tempest. "Company helps."

She nodded. "Hot chocolate, laughter, and the warm glow of the lamp—not such a bad way to weather a storm. But I have questions, if you don't mind."

He motioned for her to have a seat on the bench, and he joined her, cradling his mug in his hands. "Anything. I'd love to hear your thoughts of the past few days. You've barely said a word."

She sighed. "I'm on a voyage of exploration, William. Your lives and your family Bible have given me much to think about. So have the commentaries your parents—and you—have written within it. May I ask, who is Louise?"

William gasped. That wasn't what he thought she'd ask about. He'd deliberated about how to tell her about his ex-fiancée, but now his tongue tied in a knot as his mind raced to the intimate details of rejection he'd penned in the book. He took another sip of his cocoa, stalling for time.

"You don't have to answer, William. It's just that . . . I'd like to know how it can be as Psalm 34 says, that 'The righteous cry, and the LORD heareth, and delivereth them out of all their troubles. The LORD is nigh unto them that are of a broken heart; and saveth such as be of a contrite spirit.' "

William set his cup on the bench beside him

and took her free hand. "Louise was my fiancée. From the time we were little, our parents planned for us to marry. But God has been close to me, Julia, and He has delivered me from many troubles."

He slowly, openly shared his story of rejection and abandonment, of dreams lost and a broken heart. She listened patiently, her tangible concern giving him the courage to tell all.

When he finished, he drank the rest of his now-cold cocoa, not sure what else to say.

Thankfully, she filled the void. "I've never been engaged or even been in love, but I have felt the loss of my parents and now of Granny. But no one has ever been close to me in my pain—until you and your mother. I think, perhaps, Granny knew I could find the solace I needed here. Yet . . . delivering me from troubles? That's another matter altogether."

She slipped her hand from his and fiddled with her bracelet as if caressing it.

William touched her trinket. "I see you wear this almost every day. May I ask why?"

"It was the last thing my parents gave me before they died. It keeps them close."

He clasped her hand securely in his. "That's lovely, Julia. But regarding your troubles, I believe you're on to something. You memorized that Scripture, and those words can bring you close to God. He is the comforter, deliverer, and the Savior. Are you ready to make a change in your life?"

She shifted in her seat, a small sigh escaping her lips. "Maybe, but I still need time to think about all this, William. It's a lot to take in."

He took her hand in his and kissed it. "It's okay, my lovely Gingersnap. Keep on exploring, and you'll find your answers."

The well-tended flame brightened the lamp room, yet the shadows persisted. When would the storm outside—and inside her—pass?

Chapter 9

The past two days of clear weather brought renewed hope. In the cheerfulness of the midmorning, sunshine shimmered on the tranquil waters of the river. Julia engaged in the simple task of hanging the day's laundry, her heart brimming with contentment. She hummed a happy tune, a stark contrast to the recent storm that had mercifully given way to the embrace of the sun.

She glanced at William, just a dozen or so feet from her, immersed in the work of varnishing his boat, displaying skillfulness of hands and tools. The clinks and clatters intertwined seamlessly with nature's constant serenade of birds and bugs and waves lapping the shore. It seemed there was nothing he couldn't do.

He caught her gaze and chuckled. "That's a pretty tune, Gingersnap. I've not had the pleasure of hearing it before."

She giggled. "It's called 'Paddy's Wedding.' It's about an Irish lad who fell in love with Kitty Kelly and asked her to marry him."

"Irish, are you? I think I have a few drops of green blood in me too. In fact, Mother is making her mother's Irish soda bread as we speak."

Aunt Dee, a culinary artisan of sorts, embarked

on her weekly tradition of crafting fresh bread—Thursday's customary delight that filled the air with the comforting aroma of baking.

"Aye. My father came from Ireland when he was five, but he never spoke of his life there. Granny taught me the song and shared much about their homeland."

William chuckled. "Maybe I'll learn a few Irish tunes on my harmonica, and you can sing them."

She shrugged. "Perhaps." Truth was, she loved to sing but she hadn't since the day Granny had passed. It was as if her vocal cords had seized up. But today they felt as if they were finally awakening.

As she finished clipping the last apron onto the line, she noticed a skiff navigating the waters with an air of caution. The signs of distress were clear as the small boat swayed and rocked against the waves, contrasting with the previous serenity.

She alerted William. "What's going on with that boat? Why are they struggling so in the otherwise calm waters?"

William shielded his eyes from the sun and stared at the skiff. "I don't know, but I hope they're okay. The varnish is still wet on my skiff."

As the boat came closer to the island, the faces of worried family members came into focus—a father at the helm, a mother clutching her seat with furrowed brows, and two children peering over the sides with a mixture of confusion and anxiety.

Julia pointed to them. "I think they need help!"

She followed William to the dock, and he cupped his hands over his mouth. "Row to the dock. We'll help you."

The skiff, now precariously close to tipping, seemed caught in the relentless grip of the river's currents. The father, clearly distressed, frantically steered toward the dock.

As the skiff approached, the mother called out, "We saw your lighthouse and hoped you could help us. We've hit something, and we're taking on water."

William waved them in. "Of course, we will."

With a combination of skilled maneuvering and a touch of luck, the man guided the skiff toward the island. William and Julia lay on their stomachs and reached over the water to guide them in until the skiff bumped gently against the dock.

The father, with a blend of relief and gratitude etched on his face, climbed onto the dock followed by the rest of his family. He took the younger child's hand. "We didn't know where else to turn. We're so thankful you're here."

Julia offered a reassuring smile. "You're safe here. William will see what he can do to patch your skiff. He's a skilled boatman."

A shaggy head poked out from under a tarp in the boat—a sandy-colored dog with a playful tilt of its head. The canine broke free and wagged its tail in time with the lapping waves, teetering the damaged boat precariously.

The little boy clapped his hands, prodding the dog to exit the boat. "Come, Max."

The children burst into giggles as the dog bounded onto the dock and shook water all over them, including Julia.

The mother chuckled. "Max insisted on joining our adventure. Silly dog."

Julia swiped the wetness from her skirts, shaking her head at the romping animal. "He can dry off in the sunshine while William repairs the boat."

William put out his hand to the man. "I'm William, the lightkeeper here on Sister Island."

"I'm Alexander. This is Ruth and our children, Alan and Alice."

William inspected the skiff, assessing the extent of the damage. "Between the two of us, sir, you'll be back on the water in no time. My tools are in my workshop, so it shouldn't take but an hour or so."

Aunt Dee waved from the cottage steps. "Having a bit of trouble, folks? Welcome to Sister Island. Come. Sit on the porch and have a cold drink."

Julia led Ruth and the children to join Aunt Dee, while William and Alexander headed to the workshop. Julia poured the iced tea and offered their guests sandwiches and cookies, then took refreshments to the men too.

When she returned to the porch, Aunt Dee was engaging the family in a lively conversation, soothing their worries with tales of the river and the resilience of the island communities.

By early afternoon, the men had repaired the skiff, which now bobbed gently on the water.

As William and Alexander sipped iced tea and rested on the porch, William patted the dog's head. "Well, Max, I expect you're a seasoned sailor now."

Laughter wafted through the air as Alexander, now ready to resume their journey, expressed his thanks. "Much obliged to you all for your hospitality and help."

"Our pleasure, sir. That's why we are here. May the good Lord bless you." Aunt Dee waved them off, and Julia and William accompanied them to their boat.

Julia shared a heartfelt goodbye with the departing family. "I wish you all safe travels, including Max. Should your journey bring you back this way, remember, you're always welcome at a lighthouse."

She rested her head against the comfort of William's arm as they watched them row away. "You know, living on this island is turning out to be quite an unexpected adventure. It isn't dull or a self-imposed exile at all. I find it even more exhilarating than city life—well, at least occasionally."

He responded with a thoughtful harrumph. "Indeed, it's adventuresome at times. This summer, in particular, has brought us more excitement than usual. But there are also long and quiet stretches where the island exists in solitude. I must admit, it can get a bit lonely, even though I appreciate the peace and quiet—most of the time."

She flashed him a smile. "There's a certain charm here that's hard to resist. The tranquil moments, the drama, the breathtaking views—it's almost magical."

He chuckled. "Well, I'm glad you're finding it enchanting. It has its own kind of magic, I suppose."

Leaning in slightly, she teased, "And then, there's the company. Not everyone has the pleasure of sharing a lighthouse with someone as captivating as you."

William raised an eyebrow, a playful smirk on his lips. "Flattery will get you everywhere, Gingersnap."

She grinned, allowing her tone to take on a subtle hint. "Who knows? Maybe this island has cast its spell on me. I think, perhaps, I could get used to this life. The solitude, the river breeze, and of course, the charming lighthouse keeper."

He tentatively wrapped an arm around her shoulder. "Are you suggesting you might want to stay into the fall?"

Did he want her to? She shrugged with feigned nonchalance. "I'm just saying that there's something special about this place. And maybe, just maybe, I could see myself making it more than just a summer exile."

William's eyes held a glint of amazement, his usually composed demeanor momentarily disrupted by her words. He turned to face her. "More than just a temporary escape?"

Her heart pounded with anticipation and uncertainty in response to the hint of awe in his voice. "Maybe."

In that charged moment, his usual reserve faltered. His hand moved to gently brush a strand of hair away from her face, and she shivered. The magnetic pull between them intensified, and for a heartbeat, the world around them ceased to exist.

He tugged her closer, his breath tickling her cheek when he looked down at her. The unspoken intimacy between them hung there like a delicate thread, waiting to be acknowledged. His glance flicked to her lips, and for a fleeting instant, it appeared as though he might bridge the gap between them with a kiss.

But just as the tension reached its peak, he took a subtle step back, his gaze still locked onto hers. "You have a way of captivating me and making an ordinary moment feel extraordinary."

Though disappointed by the missed opportunity, she couldn't help but smile. "Maybe the lighthouse island magic is working its charm."

They stood side by side, the unspoken possibilities lingering in the air. And then the moment was gone. They turned away from each other and stoically watched as the skiff, now navigating the river with ease, disappeared beyond the horizon.

Julia's heart squeezed. Had she said too much and broken their bond?

Later that afternoon, William looked out at the vast expanse of the river while waiting for Julia to change and meet him for a swim. He needed to be cautious. He'd almost kissed her. The temptation to lean in and claim her lips had been tantalizingly strong, but somehow, he had managed to exercise restraint.

It wasn't easy.

Julia's journey was a spiritual one, and he didn't want to inadvertently become a hindrance on her path of self-discovery. She needed to find her own way, unencumbered by the complexities of a romantic entanglement.

His heart, though, betrayed him with its yearning. The allure of Julia's presence, the magnetic pull between them—it was both a salve for his wounded soul and a tantalizing delight. Yet he must prioritize her journey and enforce the boundaries he'd set between them.

And more than that, the pain of his own past still lingered in the recesses of his mind. The scars from his failed engagement were still healing, and he couldn't risk opening those wounds by rushing into something new. Self-preservation demanded that he tread carefully, even if his heart urged otherwise.

As Julia approached, his resolve momentarily faltered, and he waved to her. "Over here, Gingersnap!"

What a vision of loveliness! Her bathing costume reminded him of the timeless charm of the island. Julia's nautical-themed woolen outfit accentuated her curves like the river's shore. The navy-blue stripes against the cream background resembled the gentle waves of the river, a playful homage to the maritime spirit surrounding them. The fabric clung to her with a subtle elegance, leaving just enough to the imagination.

A delicately embroidered cotton top with big puffy sleeves, reminiscent of a young girl's, looked lovely on her. The crisp white fabric billowed gently in the breeze, creating an ethereal silhouette against the backdrop of the water. The knickers hinted at a sense of adventure. Beneath, bloomers that extended to right above her knees peeked out, adding a touch of modesty. Her stockings and bathing boots, made of canvas with cork soles, would protect her feet as she navigated the rocky shoreline.

He sucked in a breath and willed his eyes toward the river.

Julia joined him at the water's edge, seemingly oblivious to his overwhelmed state, and stepped into the river. "Good evening, William. The water feels marvelous." She laughed and playfully sunk her boots into the pebbly sand as she watched the gentle ripples lapping at the shore.

He grinned, a mischievous anticipation welling up inside him. "Julia, it's time you learn to swim."

She arched an eyebrow, a tangle of excitement and nervousness flickering across her face. "Swim? Me? I've never been much of a water person, though I wished I knew how the night of the collision."

He chuckled, a reassuring hand on her shoulder. "Well, that's about to change. Trust me, you're going to love it. Mother's orders. She loves swimming and wants you to experience the satisfaction of it, though her headache forbids her from joining us. Besides, if one is living on an island and helping with rescues, knowing such skills is a must."

He took her hand and led her deeper into the shallows, the cool water embracing their calves. When they were waist deep, he let go of her hand and dove in. He demonstrated a few strokes, his movements fluid and effortless. He'd always been one with the water, and he hoped she'd feel the same way one day.

After showing her the ropes, he returned to her

side. "Your turn, Julia. The key is to relax. Let the water support you."

Taking a deep breath, Julia nodded, and a hint of bravery replaced the initial hesitation on her face. With him lingering close, she tentatively stepped deeper into the water.

Step by step, he patiently guided her through the basics, teaching her how to float and tread water. Her movements were cautious at first, but as she grew accustomed to the water's embrace, confidence blossomed in her eyes.

He smiled at her progress. "See, Julia? You're a natural."

As the sun splashed a vibrant orange tint across the river and dipped lower on the horizon, he urged Julia to attempt her first strokes. With tenacity and trepidation, she pushed through the water, ripples trailing behind her.

Laughter bubbled between them, echoing across the quiet expanse of the river. Julia's initial nervousness transformed into sheer delight as she realized the freedom and exhilaration that swimming offered.

"This is amazing, William!" Her eyes sparkled, water dripping from her bathing cap. "I never thought I'd enjoy it so much."

He grinned, a shared sense of accomplishment surging between them. "I told you, Gingersnap. Mother will be so proud of you, and so am I."

As Julia grew more comfortable, the water

became a playground of laughter and splashes. A simple swimming lesson had turned into a magical memory he'd not soon forget.

When the sun fell below the horizon, they reluctantly ended their swim, tired but happy. They wrapped in towels and trudged back to the cottage, where Mother waited in the kitchen, rewarding them with hot tea and warm blueberry muffins once they changed into dry clothes.

As they gathered around the fireplace in the parlor, the flickering of the flames warmed him like the contentment enveloping him. His mother poured cups of tea, the fragrant steam rising in curls as she handed them to Julia and himself. He took a muffin from her and cradled the mug in his hands, comfort seeping through chilled fingers.

Mother opened the conversation with an impish grin. "You know, Julia, sometimes it takes a bit of courage—and a smidgen of rebellion—to discover the simple things in life. I'm glad you took that plunge."

Julia chuckled, the sound echoing in the room. "Well, it wasn't much of a rebellion, just a dip in the river. But you're right. It feels liberating to do something I was told not to."

What? William leaned back in his chair, sipping his tea. "Who disapproved of you swimming? It seems like such a harmless pleasure."

Her features turned introspective, as though memories were flashing behind her eyes. She aimlessly played with her bracelet. "They all did. Mother and Grandmother had traditional notions of propriety, I suppose. Mother believed in upholding social expectations, and Granny, bless her soul, was concerned with appearances. Swimming, for them, was a frivolous and unlady-like pursuit reserved for men, and Father didn't swim. They didn't understand the freedom and satisfaction it brings—nor did I until now."

Mother chuckled. "I attest to that. Your grand-mother *tsk*ed me when I told her of my joy of swimming."

He frowned. "It's a shame when traditions and obligations limit our experiences. But you've broken free from those constraints now."

Julia's smile widened. "Yes, and though I miss Granny and my parents, I'm beginning to realize that life is meant to be lived fully, not bound by society's obligations."

Mother sighed. "Yes, dearie. I say, live it to the full. But for now, I'm off to bed. Goodnight, you two."

For several moments after Mother left, Julia and he savored the silence. But then she asked, "When did you know you wanted to be a light-keeper?"

"Ever since my father became one, I suppose. I realized it was my calling, though, when I was still a boy."

Julia's eyes grew wide. "That young? I still

don't know what my calling is or what my future looks like. Perhaps I'll find a job somewhere. I don't know."

He gave her a reassuring smile. "You'll find your way, Gingersnap. I was twelve years old at the time, and I was still discovering the ways of the river, the secrets it held, and the lessons it would teach me. Early one evening, when Father and Mother were still away for the day, I was struggling with a bout of pleurisy. From the porch, I spied a passing tug signaling, telling me that someone on the river needed help. I ran and got into the skiff, and as I rowed in that direction, I saw an elderly fisherman. His skiff was perched on a rocky shoal, and he was fighting a losing battle against the water that rushed into his boat. He spotted me and started waving in panic."

"Goodness. And you were so young, and ill too?"

He shrugged. "Someone had to help him." Even though his lungs had screamed in protest with every pull on the oars.

"That was very brave of you." Julia sat forward. "So what happened next?"

"That day, the river became my testing ground. But in the midst of the chaos, a strange calm settled over me, and I drew upon a strength I didn't know I possessed. Somehow, I got the man into my boat. He thanked me all the way back to the mainland." William's lips tugged upward.

"On that day, I knew I wanted to follow in my father's footsteps."

"I can't blame you." Julia blew out a ragged breath. "That's quite an experience for a child, helping to save another's life. I'll never forget our rescues this summer nor the gratitude I felt at being able to serve others. There's nothing like it, is there?"

His heart warmed. "I don't reckon so, Gingersnap, but it's all the sweeter with a partner like you."

Julia grinned. "Life in the city has nothing on helping others."

He nodded. Dare he hope Julia and he would share many more adventures together?

Chapter 10

Abrisk river wind tousled Julia's hair as she walked with William the length of the island a couple of days after her swimming lesson. An approaching vessel caught her eye and halted her steps. "That boat looks official."

He tipped his chin. "Goodness! It's the lighthouse inspector. I thought he'd be coming later in the summer."

She clapped a hand over her mouth in a nervous reaction. "I think the house is ready, but I'll go and tell Aunt Dee, just in case. Be right back."

She hurried to the cottage, the distant hum of the boat's engine growing louder, heralding its approach. After she relayed the announcement to Aunt Dee, she scurried back to William's side. She'd never met an inspector and wanted to make a good first impression.

As the vessel glided toward the island, Julia squinted against the sunlight. The man in the meticulously tailored uniform standing on the steamer's deck wasn't what she'd expected. Somehow, she thought he'd be an old, seasoned sailor, but he looked as young as William.

William waved to the new arrival. "That's Lieutenant James Worthington, the new lighthouse inspector, all right. His father has been the inspector for years, but I heard James was filling in for him. I played with Jimmy as a little boy one summer when he joined his dad for the day. We had a grand time."

Julia assessed the striking figure, imagining him as a child. His cap was perfectly perched on his head, his uniform elegantly pristine, and his small, thin mustache added an air of dapper sophistication. "Boyhood pals, eh?"

William shrugged. "Just once, but it's still a fond memory."

The boat docked, and Lieutenant Worthington disembarked with the grace of a seasoned officer. When he looked at her, one raised brow suggested curiosity. A spark of amusement flickered between him and William before his gaze flitted back to her. Did he think William and she were a couple? Would her presence cause concern?

William's face broke into a wide grin, and he put out his hand to welcome the lieutenant. "Julia, this is Lieutenant Worthington, the lighthouse inspector. He makes sure everything's shipshape and shining out here." William motioned to her and smiled. "Lieutenant, this is Miss Julia Collins, a family friend who is staying with us for a while."

Julia curtsied. "Pleased to meet you, sir."

After they greeted one another, they made their way toward the cottage while the crew unloaded a boatload of supplies. Crates of kerosene for lighting the lamp and new equipment were taken to the boathouse. Fresh food, various household supplies, and even a few luxuries made their way into the cottage.

Once the crew had safely stowed the supplies, William led the inspector to the boathouse while Julia joined Aunt Dee at the kitchen table, unpacking the treasures just delivered. Julia grinned as she took in the abundance of provisions.

"Look at all this!" Aunt Dee held up a jar of pickles. "Fresh from the mainland, and they even brought me a new set of cookware."

"And these blankets . . ." Julia ran her fingers over the scratchy woolen fabric. "I can't believe how much they sent."

Aunt Dee smiled knowingly. "It's all thanks to the lighthouse board. They ensure we have what we need to keep this beacon shining bright and help where we're needed. And to stay comfortable and well-fed while we do it."

As they continued unpacking, the door creaked open, and Lieutenant Worthington stepped into the kitchen. His presence filled the room with an air of authority and purpose. He nodded to the women. "I trust the supplies arrived in good order?"

Aunt Dee curtsied. "More than adequate, thank you very much, sir. We'll have lunch ready for you at noon. I hope your inspection goes well today. We didn't expect you until later in the summer."

"Beg pardon, Mrs. Dodge. After the steamer and barge crash last month, I moved the Sister inspection up on the list to make certain you had plenty of blankets and medical supplies in case such a tragedy strikes again."

Aunt Dee tipped her chin up. "Thank you, sir. I pray that we will never need them."

Lieutenant Worthington smiled. "Agreed. Now, I'll be about my inspection and leave it to you, then. Good day, ladies."

When he had gone, Aunt Dee's attention shifted to the boxes scattered around the kitchen. "All the extras are such a blessing, don't you think?"

"It's amazing. Such a bounty." Julia pulled sacks of flour and sugar from a box.

Aunt Dee put her finger in the air, reached into the pantry, and pulled out a musty book. She opened it and placed it on the table. "This is *The Lighthouse Keepers' Manual*. We place orders from the catalog for everything under the sun." She pointed to the list in the manual, her finger tracing the neat rows of items. "Books, clothes, and daily essentials. Imagine waiting weeks or sometimes months for a delivery, not knowing if your order will arrive intact or on time. Please check off what is here. I like to keep stock of what they bring each year."

Julia read over *the annual allotment allowed*

lightkeepers in addition to the salary. " 'Two hundred pounds of pork, one hundred pounds of beef, and a generous supply of rice, beans, and peas.' Goodness."

As they worked, she ticked items that had arrived off the list, adding the extras at the bottom in her best penmanship. She chuckled as she unpacked another box, finding a peculiar assortment. Malted milk, powdered pea and beet soups, evaporated milk, and Aunt Jemima Pancake Flour. Six bottles of Coca-Cola and four bottles of Dr. Pepper clinked as she placed them on the table alongside two packages of Thomas's English muffins, neatly arranging them for Aunt Dee to put away as she knew best. Though some of the treats might not last long, the simple act of receiving a package was a cause for celebration.

Aunt Dee interrupted her musings, her tone infused with joy and gratitude. "When the boxes finally arrive, it is like Christmas morning."

Julia giggled, hugging a bottle of Coca-Cola. "It feels that way today! I never thought about the challenges that come with living on such a tiny island, but there's a special appreciation in getting these treasures. An elation I hadn't experienced in the ease of city life."

Before today, she didn't even know they were low on supplies, so in the midst of powdered soups and canned goods, she glimpsed the resilience and resourcefulness that defined Aunt

Dee—and all lightkeeping families, she supposed.

Once the older woman had stowed the supplies in their proper places, Julia and Aunt Dee turned their attention to the noon meal.

As the room grew sweltering, Aunt Dee swiped her forehead. "Open the windows, please, and let in the lovely river cross winds. We'll make Lieutenant Worthington the best shepherd's pie and blueberry buckle he's ever had. After all, we want him to feel at home, don't we?"

Julia nodded as she opened the windows at either end of the kitchen. "I'm sure it's important to make a good impression, especially for the person overseeing the lighthouse inspection."

Julia peeled potatoes as Aunt Dee diced carrots and onions, working in harmony. Soon, the aroma of sizzling meat filled the air, followed by the comforting aroma of simmering stew. The waves crashing against the rocky shore and the refreshing breeze through the windows provided a soothing ambience for their meal preparation.

Aunt Dee turned to her with a contemplative expression. "You know, Julia, life on this island is a lot like making a shepherd's pie. Layers upon layers, each ingredient adding its own flavor to the mix." She motioned toward the simmering pot on the stove, handing Julia a wooden spoon and bidding her to stir. "Faith is the foundation, the sturdy base. It's what keeps us grounded, especially when the storms roll in. And then, there's the river community—layers of relationships and shared experiences that make life all the richer."

She stirred the stew, absorbing Aunt Dee's words. How did she come up with a life lesson in everything she did? It was a gift Julia appreciated more every day.

"And our loved ones? They're like mashed potatoes on top, holding everything together. Life may seem daunting at times, but with faith and a supportive community, we can weather any storm, even the loss of our closest kin."

They worked in tandem, spooning the savory filling into the baking dish, topping it with creamy mashed potatoes. As the shepherd's pie baked, they turned their attention to the blueberry buckle. Julia blended flour and sugar and other ingredients in a bowl and then added the vibrant blueberries.

Aunt Dee inspected her work and smiled. "Life is sweet, Julia, like this blueberry buckle. Even in the toughest times, there's always a hint of sweetness if you're willing to savor it."

She'd never think of this meal . . . or life . . . the same.

William appeared in the doorway of the stifling kitchen filled with the savory aroma of his mother's cooking. "We're dining al fresco this afternoon? Smart move, Mother."

Busy at the stove, she looked over her shoulder and chuckled. "Actually, it was Julia's suggestion. The heat inside is quite relentless."

Julia gracefully made her way toward the door, a steaming dish cradled in her hands. Her silver bracelet caught the sunlight just right, momentarily blinding him. He blinked and instinctively held the door open for her while taking a generous whiff of the delectable dish as she passed. "Shepherd's pie? You spoil us, ladies." He licked his lips, memories of the comforting dish tantalizing his taste buds.

As they moved to the porch, a high noon gust of wind played with the edges of the tablecloth. It was the perfect day for an outdoor meal.

Lieutenant Worthington, leaning against the porch railing, stared out at the expansive view. A massive laker navigated the waters, a majestic spectacle against the surroundings of the tranquil island. "It never loses its charm, does it?"

In perfect sync, William and Julia responded with a shared sentiment, "Never!"

Their laughter melded with the sounds of the approaching ship.

Lieutenant Worthington joined in their merriment, a smile lifting the corners of his lips. "I must agree. There's something timeless about watching these vessels pass by. It's a reminder of the constancy in an ever-changing world."

Mother pushed the screen door open with her

backside, emerging onto the porch with a bowl of pickles and a basket of sliced sourdough bread. "Come, let's eat!"

William took the food from her and set it on the table. "Sorry, Mother, I should have gotten the door for you. The laker distracted me."

She chuckled. "They often do. That's okay."

As the four of them sat at the table, William took a moment to appreciate the simple pleasures of good company and the breathtaking scenery. Once he gave the blessing, the conversation flowed effortlessly as they filled their plates, buttered their bread, and savored the meal.

The lieutenant turned to Julia. "Well, Miss Collins. I presume you're enjoying your time here?"

Julia patted her lips with her napkin and nodded. "At first, I thought the island would be like a prison. But I'm finding my time here a life-changing experience, especially with these fine folk speaking into my life. Mrs. Dodge was my grandmother's friend, and she and William have been very kind to have me here while I see what my future holds."

Lieutenant Worthington furrowed his brows. "Do you have plans?"

A sorrowful shadow crept over her brow, so William came to her rescue. "Her granny passed recently. She's waiting for the legal matters to resolve."

The lieutenant frowned. "My condolences, miss."

Julia dipped her chin before taking a bite of the shepherd's pie. "This is delicious, Aunt Dee. What a treat! Granny made this often, though it didn't have the dash of nutmeg you added. It makes a unique taste."

Mother grinned. "Thank you, dear. It's an old family recipe. Passed down through generations."

Lieutenant Worthington helped himself to a second portion. "Well, I must say, I've never had shepherd's pie like this before either. You certainly are a great cook, ma'am."

Mother waved her hand. "Eat all you want, but it's not just the food that's special around here. It's the company too. And the view, of course."

They all laughed, their merriment punctuated by the distant hum of the laker's engines.

Lieutenant Worthington was still staring at the passing ship. "There's something about the river, isn't there? It's like a living, breathing entity, always changing but constant in its beauty."

Julia looked out at the shimmering expanse. "I never imagined I'd find such tranquility here. It's a far cry from the hustle and bustle of the city."

"I'm glad, Julia." William was pleased to see her finding comfort in their midst more each day. The shadows of sorrow she'd carried with her onto the island seemed to be slowly dissipating. But he didn't want the lieutenant to think he was smitten. William leaned toward his old friend.

"Lieutenant, do you remember coming to visit as a boy?"

The lieutenant's hearty laughter rang in the air, a rich sound infused with nostalgia. "Fond memories, indeed. Do you recall that lovely teacher who joined us?"

"Of course. She sure was pretty. What about her?"

The lieutenant leaned back, a glimmer in his eye. "Father proposed to Miss Bell, you know. But she turned him down, and I was sorely disappointed. Later that summer, I had the honor of meeting President Chester Arthur, and he taught me the art of fishing."

William raised an eyebrow in disbelief. "No kidding! What an extraordinary honor. You must cross paths with many influential people in your line of work."

The lieutenant, seemingly unfazed by the notion, nonchalantly tore apart a piece of sourdough bread. "More than you'd think, my friend. But none are more important than our dedicated lightkeepers along the St. Lawrence River." He paused, slipped the piece of bread into his mouth, and chewed before continuing. "By the way, I've been meaning to ask you—do you still spend your winters in Chippewa Bay?"

William dabbed his lips with a napkin. "Indeed, once the river freezes over. We rent a modest cabin, and I take up part-time work at the local lumberyard. Chippewa Township, as it's known, has a rich history. The government acquired the land from the Ojibwa Indians in the 1830s, but it wasn't until the Homestead Act of 1862 that settlers arrived in the area."

Mother poured more lemonade into the men's glasses. "William's father worked at a quarry in the winter. Thankfully, though, William found a safer job at the lumberyard. Pays a bit better too."

Julia, apparently surprised by the revelations, blinked several times. "I had no idea. You spend part of the year on the mainland?"

Was she pleased with that idea? Perhaps, she would consider . . . "Indeed, we do. But truth be told, I'd rather be here on the island. There's something about this place that tugs at the heart."

Lieutenant Worthington set down his fork. "Glad to hear it, William. Hey, did you hear that Michael Diepolder, the Rock Island Lightkeeper, is tying the knot in two days? Interesting twist— he's a widower with a daughter who isn't exactly thrilled about the impending nuptials."

"On July second?" Mother clapped her hands. "Well, good for him. Have you had the pleasure of meeting his bride-to-be?"

The lieutenant, chewing thoughtfully, shook his head. "No. Her name is Emma Row, she resides at Thousand Island Park, and it seems that's where the wedding bells will ring. Apparently, they've had a whirlwind romance spanning three months, and the plan is to make their home in the lighthouse after the vows are exchanged."

Mother shot William a playful, knowing grin. "Well, every lightkeeper should have a good woman at his side, don't you think?"

William huffed. What was his mother up to? She knew all too well about Julia's spiritual struggles. "In the Lord's time, of course."

Julia rose suddenly and started gathering dishes. She must've caught William's mother's implication. "I'll take care of dessert, Aunt Dee. You sit back and relax."

William sent his mother a warning glare. She'd stepped over the line this time.

Thankfully, Mother transitioned to a new line of inquiry. "How's the inspection going, may I ask?"

The lieutenant glanced toward the outbuildings. "Well, that boathouse and privy sure look splendid. The new paint improved the entire look of the island."

As Worthington continued praising their efforts around the lighthouse, Julia moved into the kitchen, but even her momentary absence annoyed William. He had to admit it—her presence felt right—she was becoming a missing piece that fit seamlessly into his life.

The idea of Julia as a lightkeeper's wife took deeper root in his mind. He envisioned her standing by his side, sharing quiet moments on the porch, watching the ships pass by, and embracing peaceful days on the island. Her smile would add a new layer of radiance to the already picturesque landscape. Her spirit, resilient and full of life, would bring a renewed energy. Infuse the routines with her own touch. Make the tasks not just chores but shared moments of purpose and unity. Together, they would tend to the beacon as it guided and brought hope to those navigating the waters.

But no. William abruptly took control of his thoughts. The harsh truth remained that she was still traversing her spiritual path of discovery, and he couldn't entertain the prospect of a romance with her until she navigated those waters.

Chapter 11

The morning sunlight filtered through the lace curtains, disbursing a cheerful brilliance on the kitchen. Julia carefully arranged the breakfast platter's stack of golden pancakes that seemed to reach for the heavens. The aroma lingered in the air, a comforting reminder of Granny's brunches. Blueberries graced a bowl like precious gems, and the aroma of sizzling bacon wafted through the air as Aunt Dee added the final touch to their breakfast banquet.

Seated at the table, Julia couldn't help but marvel at the abundance before her.

William rubbed his hands together. "What a feast!"

Aunt Dee nodded. "The supplies arrived just in time, and we've got so much more than usual. It's truly a blessing."

William blessed the food and thanked God for their freedom on this Independence Day. Once they filled their plates, he bit off a piece of bacon, swallowed, and smiled. "Julia, do you know that today is our American Independence Day?"

"Yes, your mother told me. I've never experienced your festivities, but I can't help but miss the celebrations back in Canada—which, of course, happened three days ago, on the first of the month."

William set down his coffee cup, giving her his full attention. "How does Canada celebrate?"

"Much like America does, I suppose." She expressed her fondness for Dominion Day—a celebration of grand parades, fireworks illuminating the night sky, and lively gatherings with friends and family.

He forked a piece of pancake. "Yes, sounds just like ours. Though here on the island, it's a lot quieter. We went to the Alexandria Bay celebration once, about five miles upriver, and it was quite a grand affair. But Father always had to be back before dark to light the lamp, so I've never seen fireworks."

She sighed. "That's a shame. It's my favorite part of the festivities."

Aunt Dee clicked her tongue. "Now, son, you've seen Chippewa Bay's fireworks, though they aren't nearly as nice as some."

He harrumphed, adding a little eye roll. "A few meagre ones. Nothing like they have in the cities, I'm sure." He turned to Julia. "Why do you miss your celebration so much, Gingersnap?"

"I suppose it's because I regret a mistake I made on our last Dominion Day, and I wish I could change it." Her admission, tinged with remorse and embarrassment, didn't hurt as much as she'd thought it might. The safety she experienced around the Dodges was healing her heart little by little.

William and Aunt Dee waited in silence. Taking a sip of tea, she hesitated, mindful of the eyes on her. She needed to collect her thoughts before continuing. Should she share the details of that night? Would they be disappointed in her?

Finally, she took a deep breath. "Last year, I got mixed up with the wrong crowd, and when they heard it was my birthday on Dominion Day, they planned to take me out for a celebration. They were the kinds of friends who'd use any event to be foolish, but I was too blind to see that."

Aunt Dee's concern was evident, and William leaned in, radiating understanding and empathy too. "What happened?"

She played with her pancakes, avoiding eye contact as she recounted the misguided adventure. "On my birthday, I snuck out of the house after supper. I didn't know it, but Granny had planned an after-dinner surprise party for me with fireworks to follow. As frail and sickly as she was, she had put so much effort into organizing a beautiful celebration for me, and there I was, wandering the streets with my troublemaking friends. We threw eggs at houses, and Percival yelled 'fire' at the entrance of a restaurant and ran. The boys even tied two cats' tails together and watched them fight." She blew out a breath, her words coming out in a sad confession. "I thought being with them would be a thrilling escapade, but it turned out to be reckless and foolish. In the end, it was the second-worst birthday I ever had."

"We all make mistakes," Aunt Dee said in a soft, supportive tone. "I'm sure your granny forgave you."

She shrugged, twisting her mouth to one side. "I hope so. But I ruined the entire evening, and worse, I disappointed my dear granny."

William reached his hand toward her, patting hers softly before withdrawing. "Perhaps this year's celebration will bring you new delight." His voice was also calming. "Focus on the present and embrace what the future holds. Your granny would want that."

Aunt Dee added with a small, understanding smile, "You're right, William. It's time to create fresh memories."

Julia swiped at a tear that escaped, her fork moving mechanically through the pancake stack on her plate. The memory of her past mistakes hovered in her heart, overshadowing the otherwise-peaceful meal. She looked up, meeting Aunt Dee's gaze. As reassuring as the older woman might be, doubt lingered. The pancakes, usually a delight, sat heavy in her belly. Could she truly let go of the past? Perhaps the only way she could was through the faith that the Dodges displayed. They'd been through death, trials, and other difficult things, but their lives were free of the weight she carried every day.

As they continued eating in silence, her thoughts raced. These Sister Island residents had offered peace and a respite from the chaos of her life, yet she couldn't shake the fear of the unknown. The faith and hope modeled by Aunt Dee and William were still like a distant melody, soothing yet elusive.

As if sensing her turmoil, Aunt Dee tossed her a brief smile. "My dear, it's never too late to start anew. The present is a gift, and each day is an opportunity for redemption."

Redemption? Julia looked at Aunt Dee, grappling with the conflicting emotions within her. Could she really embrace a new day, unburdened by the shadows of yesterday?

William cleared his throat. "You said that was your second-worst birthday. May I ask about your first?"

She shuddered inside, the memory of it plunging her into emotions she'd kept at bay for far too long. Tears threatened at the back of her eyelids, but she blinked them back. She'd never told anyone the tale—not her parents nor her granny. But somehow, she felt safe to unload the sad memory.

She swallowed, setting down her fork. "It was my tenth birthday. Mother invited two of her socialite friends' sons to celebrate with me while the women played cards and talked. It wasn't really a birthday party for me as much as an excuse for Mother to be with her friends." She kept her voice low, experiencing the fragility of spirit from all those years ago, but a tinge of bitterness tainted her words.

William extended a comforting hand across the table, silently offering strength.

She drew a breath, exhaled, then continued. "Percival and Frederick were incorrigible. They made up a game to chase me all over the house and outside in the yard, and every time they caught me, they kissed me, laughing and saying mean things to me. After what seemed an eternity, I finally ran to the attic and hid inside a steamer trunk." She traced the patterns on the tablecloth. "I fell asleep inside it, hoping that when I woke up, it would all be a bad dream. But reality was harsh."

The kitchen felt like a confessional, a safe and sacred space to unburden her pain. Memories long confined found a voice, and the vulnerability she exposed cut through the quiet. The import of her words settled, and a tear finally escaped, running a solitary path down her cheek. She brushed it away with the back of her hand.

"My mother's anger was swift and merciless. She scolded me for ruining her plans, for not entertaining her guests properly. And then, to punctuate the lesson, she took the porcelain doll Granny had given me and gave it away."

Julia fidgeted with the edge of her napkin. The room, once filled with the aroma of breakfast, now held the lingering scent of a painful past. "After that day, I learned to wear a mask to please others. I buried any pain or disappointment, convincing myself that I was the stronger for it. But I suppose that's why I turned to that rowdy crowd. As a little bit of rebellion, but also to be accepted."

Aunt Dee grasped her other hand, bringing even more comfort.

William's hand gently squeezed hers, a muted acknowledgment of the strength it took to revisit such wounds.

As she looked up, a glimmer of something pressed her beyond the pain—a fresh understanding and acceptance—urging her to break free from the shackles of a past that had defined her for too long.

But could she? That was the question of the summer.

William embraced the early-morning hours, the gentle swirl of the beacon illuminating the darkness and filtering through the glass. He sat on the weathered bench in the lamp room, the scrape of his whittling knife against wood creating a soothing cadence in the quiet space. The scent of fresh pine filled the air as he meticulously carved a belated birthday gift for Julia, a labor of love born from a desire to mend the fractures in her wounded soul. He prayed that his humble creation would bring her happiness and help heal the scars of birthdays past.

As the sound of footsteps resonated on the lighthouse ladder, he instinctively hid his carving, fearing an early arrival from Julia. To his surprise, his mother's silvery-white hair appeared, and he rushed to assist her up and into the room, welcoming her to his quiet refuge.

"Good morning, son." Mother's expression sparked with enthusiasm. "I think we should plan Julia a memorable belated birthday celebration. I've tossed and turned half the night fretting over the poor girl, but I have an idea."

He nodded, pulling out the almost-completed carving. "I agree. I've been working on this." He presented the wooden plaque, the inscription taking shape with the words *You are loved—God*, the *O*s crafted in the form of hearts.

Mother ran a gentle finger over the carving. "This is beautiful, son. You're a good man, and talented. Thank you for thinking of her. Now, to make it a surprise, what I need from you is to take her on a long boat trip. I want to bake a cake and prepare a special meal. Can you do that, please?"

He grinned. "What a great idea! I'd love to. And after, I'll give her a concert."

Hopefully, he and his mother would create happy memories and dispel the bad. And maybe, just maybe, he could do that for her for the rest of her life.

An hour later, William entered the kitchen where Mother had set out a simple yet scrumptious breakfast of French toast and sausage. He had finished the plaque just in time.

When Julia joined them, she put her hands over her mouth and giggled with glee. "French toast is my favorite! Thank you for such a lovely meal and your gracious hospitality. I feel like family here, more than I ever did growing up. You two are the best."

"I love you, dearie." Mother hugged her before pulling out the chair for her to sit.

If only William could be so free and say the same . . .

After his mother took her place and said the prayer, William reached for his coffee cup as he bestowed a smile on Julia. "May I have the honor of showing you some of the islands around here this fine morning? Except for a few rescue runs, you haven't been off this patch of earth in over six weeks. How about it?"

Julia clapped her hands like a happy child. "I'd love to. That'd be grand, William."

After breakfast, he escorted Julia to the skiff, and they set sail. The small vessel glided across the waters, weaving through the tapestry of the Thousand Islands. Brothers Islands, Hemlock Island, Halfway Island—all unveiled their charms under the morning sun, their stories whispered by the lapping waves. And shared by him.

Julia turned to him with a thoughtful expression. "William." Her voice carried a hint of curiosity. "Tell me more about your beliefs. About the God you say you know so well."

Feeling the gravity of the question, he met Julia's gaze with a gentle sincerity. This conversation was not just about theology—it was an exploration of the soul, a chance to bridge the gaps in understanding.

"Well," he began, choosing his words with care, "I believe in the Creator God, the Lord of the universe who shapes and infuses us and our world with purpose and beauty. It brings me comfort to know there's Someone bigger than me who guides my actions."

Julia nodded, a river breeze tousling her hair. "But how do you *know* there's a Creator?"

William paused, contemplating how to convey the depth of his conviction. "For me, it's like seeing the details of a painting. The symmetry, the order, the complexity—it all points to a masterful artist behind the masterpiece. I find that same sense of awe and wonder when I look at His creation all around me."

Julia's eyes searched his as if seeking to understand the essence of his faith. "And God? How does He fit into your life?"

William smiled. "God—the Father, Son, and Spirit—is the essence of love and compassion. He's the guiding force that connects us all, the source of grace and redemption. I find comfort in the reality that we are all part of His larger, loving plan. He is my everything, Julia."

A silence settled between them, the gentle lull of the boat creating a cradle for contemplation. Julia was clearly absorbing his words, and their conversation seemed to deepen with each revelation.

"But what about when bad things happen?" Her brow furrowed with the weight of a world of uncertainties.

He stopped paddling, allowing the boat to float on the river's current. "That's a question many grapple with. I believe that even in the face of adversity, there's an underlying purpose, a greater good that may not always be clear to us at the moment. But faith is a journey, and part of it is finding the strength to navigate the storms with resilience and hope."

"I . . . I think I see." Julia's face, once filled with doubt, then with curiosity, now held a hint of deep introspection.

As they continued their journey, several boats and a laker passed them. They continued on a leisurely course, the sun shining bright upon the water. The mingling scents of musk and pine and the distant laughter of seagulls added a playful melody to the tranquil scene.

Julia had shifted the conversation to lighter topics, and he let her lead, sensing she needed a reprieve from the deeper things she'd asked of him. They laughed and shared stories, waved at boaters, and simply enjoyed being together.

By midday, William glided the boat smoothly to the dock. The inviting aromas of Mother's cooking wafted through the air, creating a delicious prelude to the feast that awaited.

Mother, with flour-dusted hands and a kind smile, welcomed them into her culinary haven. Pots simmered on the stove, sending fragrant whispers of herbs and spices into the air. The table, adorned with carefully arranged dishes, awaited the eager guests.

Mother beckoned them to the table. "Happy belated birthday! Come, come, let's celebrate Julia on this special day."

Julia's hands flew to her cheeks, tears welling up in her sweet ginger eyes. "For me?"

He and mother laughed at her happy response as he offered his arm to escort her to her celebration. Each bite of that meal was a revelation—a burst of savory or sweet, a synthesis of textures and aromas. The summer sunlight streaming through the windows added a warming touch. And the birthday cake, adorned with delicate frosting and candles, took center stage.

As Julia took the first taste, she closed her eyes and savored the confection. He joined her, the flavors melding on his palate, a harmonious blend of sweetness.

When William gave her his gift of the carving, Julia wrapped her arms around his neck in thanks, setting his heart to dance. But she quickly pulled back, apologizing for her actions. Her eyes snapped toward his mother in alarm.

Mother waved off her concerns, handing her a gift wrapped in brown paper and tied with a bow. "I hope you like them."

Julia opened the package containing the tatted collar and cuffs his mother had been working on for so long. "Thank you! These are beautiful. I'll treasure them always."

Around the table, laughter rang like a melody, the amiable flush of friendship warming the room.

Julia raised her glass in gratitude. "Thank you for everything. This day has been a healing embrace—one that replaces the bad memories of birthdays past with the promise of a brighter future."

Mother raised her glass too. "It's our pleasure, dearie. Today is about creating new memories, ones that will linger in your heart like the aroma of a cherished meal."

As the afternoon waned into the evening, William added a few new memories of his own. Ones of music, celebration, and hope. Perhaps there was a lifetime of new memories on the horizon.

Chapter 12

After a peaceful week of basking in the solitude of the island and contemplating the deep things of faith, Julia hurried to join William by the shore as he waved at a boat approaching from the American mainland. Aunt Dee followed her, picking up her skirts and laughing gleefully. But who was this?

The couple in the boat had to be in their forties and the girl with them not yet a teener. The prospect of any visitor gracing their secluded haven was always a cause for curiosity. Yet the way William bounced on the balls of his feet and the high pitch of Aunt Dee's giggle suggested these particular arrivals were no ordinary guests.

"Well, I'll be." William caught Julia's eye and gestured toward the approaching boat, a huge grin lighting his face. "It's none other than the Rock Island lightkeeper, Michael Diepolder, who Lieutenant Worthington mentioned. He was a friend of my father's for years. And that must be his daughter, Ada. She would be about eleven, right, Mother?"

Aunt Dee nodded solemnly. "Her mother passed away a few years ago, and Michael has been caring for her on his own ever since, poor man.

I've often wondered how they've been faring. I reckon that's his new bride the inspector spoke about. It'll be grand to meet her."

But the arrival of her hosts' friends stirred a complex brew of emotions within Julia. Until now, their island visitors, except for the inspector, had all been strangers, allowing her to feel an inherent sense of belonging and acceptance. As if she were an important part of the family. Yet now, she found herself feeling that she might suddenly become the outsider, and she didn't like it one bit.

A twinge of loneliness crept over her, prompting tears to well up behind her eyelids. She blinked them back, questioning the validity of her perceived belonging. The idea of her being the stranger in the group took hold. Perhaps she should withdraw to her room, allowing the others to engage in conversation without her.

"Dee. William. It's been far too long," the man called out, his voice filled with a combination of happiness and nostalgia. "A lightkeeper gets too few days off, but I had to bring my wife to meet you."

The woman and girl waved tentatively, the lady holding her hat on her head, one eyebrow raised, while the girl glanced at her father as though seeking his approval on whether to be friendly or not. As they chugged nearer, they stared at Julia with questioning expressions.

She hesitated as the unfamiliar figures set foot on the island, observing from a distance while her friends embraced and exchanged effusive greetings with the woman. Julia couldn't shake the overwhelming sense of displacement, akin to that of a lost child yearning to seek refuge behind the comforting shelter of her father's coattails. Or an orphan wishing for family.

The scene transported her back to the familiar discomfort she had endured numerous times in the past. Memories surfaced of her mother's gatherings with high-society friends when she was a young girl who felt like a mere shadow—invisible, undesired, and, at times, deemed a nuisance. The sting of being dismissed cut deep, and she feared it might happen again.

Sometimes, though, the wounds of rejection had found comfort on the rare occasions when her father was home. During those moments, he would invite her into his office to play checkers or chess and discuss nature, enveloping her in a cocoon of love that contrasted starkly with her mother's habitual dismissals. Maybe the Dodges would do the same today.

"Julia? Come over here, dear. I'd like you to meet some cherished friends of ours." Aunt Dee beckoned for her to join the gathering, and she complied, suppressing the bitter memories that clouded her thoughts and emotions.

It took effort, but she adorned her face with a

smile and gave the newcomers a small curtsy. "Hello."

Oh, dear! Had they noticed her tone? Even to her own ears, it carried a hint of childlike reticence.

William stepped closer to her, placing his hand on her forearm. "Julia, I'd like you to meet the Rock Island lightkeeper, Michael Diepolder, his daughter, Ada, and his new bride, Mrs. Emma Diepolder." His touch offered a comforting anchor, and she found strength in the reassuring pat he gifted her. His encouraging smile accompanied the introduction. "And this, my friends, is Julia Collins, a dear family friend who is gracing us with her presence for the summer."

Mrs. Diepolder seemed to be caught in a moment of contemplation, but she gently took both of Julia's hands into her own. The woman stared at her face with a cross between confusion and curiosity. What was the woman thinking? A shiver crept down Julia's spine under the depth of her scrutiny.

"You look so much like someone I once knew and loved deeply." The older woman's voice cracked with a touch of melancholy. "Your vibrant ginger eyes, just like hers. Your smile . . . I miss her." A shadow of sadness flickered in her eyes, leaving Julia at a loss for words.

"I'm sorry for your loss, missus." Swallowing her dismay, Julia shifted her attention to the young girl at her father's side. "Ada, is it? You're a pretty little thing."

The child must have sensed an undercurrent of discomfort between Mrs. Diepolder and herself, for she clung tightly to her father's hand. Her wide eyes darted between the women, and her nose wrinkled. "I'm not little or a thing. I'm eleven." She dismissed both the words and Julia with a huff and turned her attention to the cottage. "This lighthouse is much different than ours, Papa."

In the wake of Ada's declaration, an uneasy silence settled over the group.

Julia, sensing the need to defuse the tension, mustered a friendly smile. "Eleven is a lovely age. You have so many exciting adventures ahead of you."

Mrs. Diepolder's gaze lingered on Julia for a moment longer before she released her hands with a gentle pat. "Indeed. Children bring such merriment into our lives."

William turned to the girl, bent a little, and placed his hands on his knees. "Ada, would you like to explore our island a little? I've been to Rock Island a time or two, and though the lighthouses may be similar, this island is quite different from yours."

Ada's eyes lit up with curiosity. "Oh, I would, very much."

William smiled. "After lunch, then."

As they headed to the cottage, the group exchanged trivialities and observations, gradually bridging the gap between familiarity and the unknown. Julia found herself caught between the conflicting currents of past wounds and the prospect of new connections.

Silent until now, Mr. Diepolder addressed William.

"We heard about the tragedy that occurred June the seventh—the collision between the steamer and the barge. I read about it in the papers a little over a month ago. As lightkeepers, I believe it's important to review such events so we can improve our rescue techniques for the future, don't you think?"

William extended a hand toward the kitchen porch. "Absolutely. Join me."

While the men sat on the porch and delved into a discussion about the crash, bonding as fellow lightkeepers, the women took charge of preparing lunch. Aunt Dee supervised as Julia, Mrs. Diepolder, and even Ada pitched in to chop, slice, and dice ingredients for what promised to be a delightful chicken salad.

Aunt Dee paused in dicing an onion to swipe the tears running down her cheeks with her sleeve. "The journey from Rock Island must have been quite a trek. However did you manage it?"

To Julia's surprise, Ada responded. "We borrowed a wagon, drove to Chippewa Falls, and took the boat from there. It was quite an adventure, and we have to do it all over on the way home."

Aunt Dee chuckled. "That's right, dear. Say, we grownups can handle things here. Feel free to go and explore a bit before lunch."

Ada glanced at Mrs. Diepolder, who gave her a nod. "Go ahead, honey."

When the girl fled the cottage, Mrs. Diepolder cocked her head, her furrowed brow begging information. "Where are you from, Julia?"

"Brockville, in Canada. Do you know it?"

The knife slipped from Mrs. Diepolder's grasp, producing a sharp clang on the cutting board that reverberated like an alarm. She gasped, and her hands flew up to cover her mouth, her eyes widening. "I knew it! You're Myrtle's daughter, aren't you?"

Julia's heart took to trotting, and she almost dropped the pickle jar she was holding. "You knew my mother? How?"

Mrs. Diepolder hurried over to her and hugged her tightly. When she pulled away, her eyes glistened with tears. "I'm your Aunt Emma, Julia, your mother's sister. I moved to Thousand Island Park years ago, and we . . . well . . . my sister and I have been disenfranchised for ages."

What was happening? It couldn't be true!

A boulder-sized lump stuck in Julia's throat until she could hardly breathe. She set the jar on the table and grasped the edges of it. Her mother had never mentioned a sister named Emma.

Aunt Dee wiped her hands on her apron. "Goodness gracious! How providential! Why don't you two go into the parlor and talk in private? I'll finish up here."

Following Aunt Dee's suggestion, Julia staggered to the settee and plunked down as Mrs. Diepolder—her aunt?—joined her. Julia's insides shook like a leaf, and she swallowed several times to dislodge the lump that threatened to remain in her throat.

How could she start a conversation with an aunt she didn't know? What should she admit about her mother, her family? "My parents . . . they refused to speak of the past. Granny too. I knew only that my mother had three sisters who lived in America."

Aunt Emma fixed a kindly expression on her. "I'm sad to say that I didn't even know about you. I knew Myrtle married, but then we stopped talking, and I deeply regret that. How are your parents? Do you have siblings?"

A flood of sad memories filled her thoughts. "They died in a boating accident when I was fourteen. It's just me."

Julia's aunt extended a hand toward her, but she drew hers close, wringing them nervously. This was all too overwhelming. For both of them, surely.

Aunt Emma seemed to understand, for her brows furrowed compassionately. She folded her hands and placed them in her lap. "Oh, Julia! I'm so sorry for your loss. I wish I had known. When our parents discovered that our sister Lucy was expecting a child outside of marriage, our family faced a severe rift, causing loyalties to splinter and relationships to fray. Lucy was sent away. But after that, none of us knew what happened to her. I wanted to find her, to support her, but the others . . . well, it was an embarrassment to our family and a topic we were banned from speaking about. Then, when your parents married, your mother refused to engage with any of us, so I just stayed away to keep the peace. The entire terrible situation tore our family apart, and I've mourned it to this day."

Julia gasped, her pulse thumping in her temples. Her aunt's words tumbled in her brain. "What are you talking about?"

Slowly and carefully, her aunt told Lucy's tragic story. A sailor taking advantage of her. Her parents rejecting her, banishing her in shame. The baby girl she named Libby, adopted by another family.

Julia took a deep breath. So that was why Mother had kept it all a mystery. Time had woven deep and shameful fractures into their family tree. What other skeletons did her parents keep from her? Why hadn't her granny told her about this?

175

Aunt Emma reached out to take her hands, and this time, Julia accepted the tender gesture. "I'm so sorry, Julia. There's so much your mother and I never said, so many wounds left to fester in silence. We were separated from one another by circumstances and social bias. When she married and I moved to America, the chasm grew even larger, so we both just went on with our lives, I suppose."

Julia's eyes welled with tears, the reality of the revelation settling on her shoulders.

Aunt Emma drew her into a hug, a reassuring reminder that they were close relations. "We can't change the past, Julia, but what we can do is face it, acknowledge the pain, and hopefully, forgive all the wrongs. And we can be family now. Let's write to each other and find a way to spend time together, okay?"

Julia simply nodded, wiping away the tears that slid down her cheeks. Though it was comforting to know she suddenly had family in her life, how could she forgive her parents and Granny's secrecy? How could she move forward without the pain?

William sat beside Julia on the porch as the afternoon breeze gently stirred the air, carrying with it a sense of peace. He marveled at the unexpected relationship between Julia and Mrs. Diepolder—blood ties declared, family roots uncovered. Pain exposed. And hopefully soon, hearts healed.

As the Diepolders embarked on their journey back to the mainland, William's mother sought rest in her room, succumbing to the weariness that followed the day's festivities. As usual, she had thrown herself into entertaining, a testament to the depth of care and connection she felt with her friends.

William sensed that Julia needed to talk about the whirlwind of emotions that must have swept through her. But for now, she appeared distant and contemplative. The events of the day were undeniably life-changing for her. Should he bridge the gap and press her to share?

He said a quick prayer for wisdom, then he took her hand and squeezed it. "This has been quite a day for you, I expect. It's a lot, isn't it?"

She sighed, the sound a combination of exhaustion and contemplation, he guessed. "It is, William. I thought I was an orphan. I never imagined finding family, let alone in such a strange way here on this island. It's like a novel unfolding, and I'm not sure where the next chapter leads."

He nodded, understanding the perplexity of her emotions. "Sometimes our journey takes unexpected turns, and we are forced to face chapters we never anticipated. But in those moments, we also discover a new resilience within us. The strength to navigate the unknown. The faith to move forward. You're a strong woman, Julia. You'll find your way."

Julia's quivering sigh carried traces of sorrow and longing. "My parents avoided any discussion of family or faith. They only ever spoke of social endeavors, my father's work, or the gossip they read in the newspaper or heard on the streets. They fought all the time, and I never once heard them forgive each other or even say they were sorry. It was as if apologies and forgiveness were foreign concepts to them, so I don't really know how all that works."

Slowly, she unveiled the layers of her past. "My mother was very religious and always went to church. She did good deeds with her church for the community, and she made me attend services with her. But whenever I got bored and looked around or wiggled in my seat, she'd pinch me." Her pain lingered in the air, a palpable sting of both physical and emotional pain. "Then, all the way home, she'd scold and ridicule me for being a wicked heathen."

She shifted in her seat and fidgeted nervously.

William scooted his chair closer to her, placing his arm around her shoulder, offering a supportive presence without interrupting the flow of her story.

Julia glanced at his extended arm and took a deep breath before continuing. "When I was eight, thanks to Granny, I gave my heart to God at a church service. I felt His loving kindness and sensed His presence. But my mother scoffed at my experience and forbid me to go to church with Granny again. By the time I was ten, I begged my father to let me stop going to church with Mother, and he prevailed."

A heaviness settled in the silence that followed. How could parents be so cruel? His heart wrenched at the thought.

"It must have been so difficult for you," he acknowledged tenderly, "to navigate faith and family and all the expectations placed upon you."

Julia nodded, sorrow evident on her face. "I always felt like an outsider in Mother's church, as though I didn't belong. It left me with this strange relationship with faith—something I associated with judgment and criticism rather than the peace and hope you and your mother have."

A quiet sadness lingered in her teary eyes as she continued. "I was never allowed to ask about family. The topic was off-limits, and even Granny refused to enlighten me, even after my parents passed. By then, I'd learned to not even ask about it. Aunt Emma told me more about our family than I ever knew, and I look forward to talking with her more."

He listened, but his heart ached over the pain she carried. With his free hand, he squeezed hers gently. "I'm glad you and your aunt connected,

Julia. But know this, in our family, there's never a topic that's off-limits. You can ask Mother and me anything."

Julia stared at the sky, where puffy clouds scurried across the vast expanse. The moment held a quiet intensity. "Since you mention it, I need to know something. How can you forgive someone who's already died? I'm so mad at my mother for the way she kept me out of her life, and angry at my parents and Granny for keeping my aunts from me."

The depth of Julia's pain and her longing for understanding pressed on his chest. He prayed again and chose his words carefully. "Forgiveness is a journey, Julia. It's not about condoning the wrong or forgetting what happened. It's about giving the offense to God and allowing Him to fill your life with peace. It's acknowledging the pain, the anger, and allowing yourself to let it go. Then it's making hundreds of choices after that to keep on forgiving. Your mother's choices may have hurt you, and it's okay to be mad. Your parents' and Granny's silence hurts too. But forgiving them is a gift you give yourself, a release from carrying the load of that anger. It takes time, but if you ask God for help, He can help you in that journey. And I'm here for you as well, every step of the way."

"Thank you, William. That means a great deal to me."

Dare he speak about her father's philosophy she embraced as faith? Her father's ideas wouldn't help her heal. Only God could.

"Julia, I know your father felt there was no need for faith in the traditional sense, and that he felt nature was sufficient as the only intellectual and spiritual experience he needed. How did you come to adhere to that?"

Julia stared at the river. "It was safe. Comforting. My father believed in the beauty and power of the natural world, while Mother sought control through religion. For him, it was about connecting with the earth—and that never hurt. But now . . ."

William nodded, finally understanding her mindset. "It's an interesting perspective, to find a safe spirituality in the natural world, especially since your mother's faith hurt you."

A faint smile touched Julia's lips. "I hadn't really thought about it like that. My mother's faith was so gray, so empty. I thought the idea of God, the Trinity, and a Savior were silly superstitions. For her, they were devoid of life. But for you and Aunt Dee? I'm beginning to wonder if it depends on how each person applies faith—or not."

William's pulse ticked up. "Exactly. You can do all the religious things and go through all the motions, but unless you actively engage in a relationship with God, it's only duty. Religion. As you say, it's gray. Empty. Boring. Useless.

But when you embark on a personal, vibrant relationship with Him, it's as marvelous as seeing a triple rainbow for the first time."

The metaphor lingered in the night air, and William prayed it would help her understand.

Julia licked her lips. "So faith is not merely a set of rituals but a living, breathing relationship? That's new to me."

William kissed her hand. "It is, Julia. It really is."

He held back the question that burned in his chest. *Will you pray with me?* He sensed she still needed time, but how long would it take?

Patience, William. Patience.

Chapter 13

A week after the Diepolders' visit, Julia stood on the weathered dock, surveying the distant line where the sky met the river. A building storm in the north mocked the tumultuous emotions swirling within her. A full-blown war had begun, a battle between her father's ideas and the beliefs she beheld here on the island. She just wasn't sure which would be the victor.

And her aunt's counsel to forgive? That was still a mystery yet to be solved.

As the wind picked up and the steady lapping of the waves turned irregular, a low hum in the distance disrupted her musings. Julia squinted into the sunlight to discern the source. A luxurious steamer yacht emerged from the hazy mirage, its polished exterior gleaming like a jewel on the water.

The engine's purr grew louder, pulling Julia from the depths of her contemplation. The yacht gracefully approached the dock, cutting through the choppy waves with precision, dwarfing the small island pier. Its sleek design spoke of affluence, a vessel accustomed to navigating the exclusive waters of privilege. A crew member, dressed in crisp maritime attire, secured the yacht to the dock with practiced ease.

Who could be coming here in such a vessel, and on such a day?

A swelling thunderhead and gust of wind rocked the boat, creating an unsteady wriggle between water and vessel. Julia's curiosity grew, and she stepped closer.

The yacht's door swung open, presenting a tall figure stepping from the shadows onto the deck. A man of sophistication, his fine fedora and tailored suit bespoke opulence. His eyes met Julia's, and a subtle smile played upon his lips.

Julia gasped, stepping back in disbelief.

Percival Stevenson? Impossible.

The man belonged to the most influential family in Brockville. The son of one of Mother's high-society acquaintances, he had, on several occasions, been projected as her potential future husband. After Percival had played a part in her two birthday nightmares, Julia had written him off as trouble and an insufferable bore, even after he apologized for the fiascos and tried to be nice when they were teens.

"My darling Julia." His voice—velvety, yet filled with his usual hubris—caused her skin to crawl. "You're a hard one to track down. When I heard about your grandmother and discovered she'd imprisoned you on this desolate island, I knew I had to rescue you."

She blinked twice. "Rescue me?"

Percival stepped onto the dock and grasped

her hand. "I can't pretend to understand why you're in this place, but I can imagine the pain that brought you here, and I'm sorry that you lost your grandmother. But Julia, I see my future with you by my side, and I want you to come back to Brockville and marry me. My family has said they would welcome you into our fold."

Her mind raced through the memories—her mother's insufferable demands. The scheme hatched by their mothers, planning the future union of Percival and herself even when they were at the tender age of fourteen. They had laughed about it at the time, but now he wanted to go through with it? She compared her losses and the emptiness to the moments of pure delight she had found on the island. A tear welled up in her eye as she cringed at the proposition before her.

Here on Sister Island, she'd been free from the constraints of societal expectations and the judgmental glares of those who once dismissed her as an orphan. But now, faced with the allure to join a prestigious family with position in the community and have everything she ever dreamed of, a wave of conflicting emotions crashed over her.

But only for a moment.

She squared her shoulders and raised her chin. "No, Percival. I will not go back with you, nor will I marry you. This summer on the island was

Grandmother's idea, and I intend to honor it to the very end. Besides, why me? You hardly know me."

"You know what our mothers intended, and I agree with their wisdom." Percival reached out to touch her cheek, but she backed away. He reached for her other hand, but she tugged both of hers from his, plunging them into her apron pockets.

Undeterred, he continued, sweeping a hand toward his yacht. "Just imagine what we could build together. You'd have a life of ease. A life beyond anything you've ever imagined."

Julia shut her eyes, for a split second caught again in the conflict between the enticement of a financially stable future and the precious connections she was establishing in this place. Adding to this, the spiritual battles she had been grappling with and the building storm around her that emulated the turmoil within her heart. As if to shake her into reality, a loud thunderclap rumbled on the river.

She jumped. "No, Percival. No!" She surprised herself with her strong, steady response. "You heard what I said. I meant it."

His brow lowering, Percival glanced at the impending storm and then beyond her as William sprinted to her side, coughing and trying to catch his breath.

After several moments, William cleared his

throat and wheezed. "Who's our visitor? Do you know him?"

Julia scooted closer to William. "He's an acquaintance from Brockville."

Percival shook his head, scowling at William. "I am not an acquaintance. I came to take her home and marry her." He spoke in a firm tone as if the matter were already settled.

William's eyes grew wide, and he wheezed again, falling into another coughing fit. "Marry her?"

Julia touched his forearm. "He asked me, but I am not going with him. I'm here for the summer, just as Granny wished. Goodbye, Percival."

Julia walked away, tugging William to follow, leaving Percival alone on the dock.

Not surprisingly, Percival had to have the last word. "You'll change your mind—I'm sure of it. I'll be back in a month and will expect an affirmative answer, Julia. Your grandmother would've wanted this for you. Your parents too. Don't disappoint them. Or me."

She refused to turn around or respond, continuing her headlong scurry to the cottage, fleeing the scene with William close on her heels.

When she entered the kitchen, Aunt Dee waited at the table, which was set with tea and scones, fresh fruit, and sliced tomatoes. "Who in heaven's name was that?"

Julia plunked down and hid her face in her hands.

William sat next to her. "A beau who asked for her hand."

Julia slapped her hands on the table. "He's not my beau, William! He's a cavalier cad who thinks he can have anything he wants."

William's brow furrowed. "Why did he think you would marry him?"

Goodness! She had to make them both understand. As thunder rumbled and lightning flashed, she told them about their mothers' scheme. His proposal. Her refusal.

When she finished, Aunt Dee took her hand and squeezed it. "Oh dearie, what a difficult position he put you in. Do you really think your granny and parents would want you to marry a man like that, even though he's wealthy? There's so much more to life than money, you know."

She shook her head. "Mother might have, but that doesn't matter. I refused him and am glad of it."

She had just made a decision that would shape the course of her life. Had she been too impulsive? Should she have considered the options and their consequences longer?

The air in the room pressed down as Aunt Dee frowned, her eyes betraying deep concern. The flickering candlelight tossed shadows on the walls, creating an atmosphere of somber reflection as the storms raged.

William cleared his throat once more while

ladling a generous amount of honey into his tea, swirling it with his spoon. The scowl on his face intensified, now tinged with sadness and bewilderment. But he said nothing. He just sipped his tea.

"It's time to tell you something, Julia." Aunt Dee's voice, soft and full of empathy, soothed her confused mind. "It's about that afternoon— the day your parents went boating and died."

Swallowing hard, Julia met her gaze. The memory of that tragic day had haunted her for years, a burden she carried alone.

"I saw them, Julia." Aunt Dee's eyes brimmed with unshed tears. "I saw them just hours before they died. They came here, and we had a conversation about you. That is one of the reasons your grandmother wanted you to sojourn here. To hear the whole story from my lips."

Julia's breath caught in her throat. The room closed in around her as she waited for Aunt Dee to unveil the details that had remained shrouded in mystery.

"They weren't angry at you, Julia. They were worried about you." Aunt Dee's voice trembled. "They said you had an argument and refused to go on the boat trip with them. But they weren't upset with you. They were concerned about your future, for the choices you were making. And now, my dear girl, you have some really huge decisions ahead of you."

A deep sob escaped her lips. Tears spilled down her cheeks as the truth unfolded. Her guilt shifted, replaced by a new understanding.

William took her hand and held it. A wave of security enveloped her.

"I blamed myself for so long." Julia whispered, her voice choking past the lump in her throat. "I thought if I had only gone with them, then maybe . . ."

Aunt Dee reached across the table, taking Julia's other hand in hers. "No, sweetheart. The accident wasn't your fault. And no matter how flawed their views and intentions might have been, they loved you deeply, and their concern for you was born out of that love. Your father and your mother wanted only the best for you, and they believed in the strength within you to one day make the right choices."

As Julia absorbed the revelation, a mosaic of emotions surged within her—sorrow, relief, and a newfound appreciation for the depth of her parents' love. She lovingly touched her bracelet, wishing she could caress the givers of it.

"They knew they couldn't control every aspect of your life, though they struggled with it," Aunt Dee continued, her tone tender. "But they trusted in your ability to navigate the world well, even if they couldn't be there with you. And now, you can show them and the world that they were right."

Julia's tears flowed freely now, of grief for her loss and gratitude for the truth that had finally come to light. William let go of her hand and gave her his handkerchief while Aunt Dee released her other hand and brushed tears from her cheeks. Each offered a comforting presence in the midst of the emotional storm.

A dazzling burst of light lit the room, and her teacup trembled beneath a mighty thunderclap. She took a deep breath and sighed, letting out a lifetime of angst and regret.

Aunt Dee raised an eyebrow and poured some tea. "Drink, Julia. It's time to release yourself from the burden of guilt and allow your parents' love—and your granny's, too—to guide you forward to make wise decisions about your future."

In that intimate moment, Julia felt a sense of closure—and the beginning of a journey toward healing. The truth had set her free from the chains of self-recrimination, and the love of her parents, though gone, would live on as a guiding light in her heart.

But still, so many decisions had settled upon her shoulders. The island had become a place of healing and self-discovery. Could she forgive them—and herself—and embrace a faith that would turn her world upside down?

William sat across the table from his mother and Julia, and the oppressive mugginess pressed against his chest like an invisible force, each breath a sharp reminder of the pleurisy that had again taken hold.

Not now! Twice in one summer? That hadn't happened since he was a boy.

In the preceding hours, the ordeal had begun with an abrupt, piercing pain seizing his chest—a relentless interloper that grew more agonizing with each breath. And just when he thought the day couldn't get any worse or take a more unexpected turn, that Brockville blue-blood came calling—for *his* Gingersnap!

The man had obviously been one with significant influence. And he wasn't just any suitor—he was a family friend, boldly declaring that the union was not just his desire but a predestined wish of her deceased parents and even her granny. After further consideration, would Julia renege and accept his offer?

William wanted her. He admitted it. But she was still on a journey he'd not derail, even if she crushed his dreams. As a simple lightkeeper, with little to offer her now or in the future, how could he dare dream of competing with such a formidable opponent as that man with a yacht?

His hands trembled as he reached for the small jar of honey on the kitchen table. He assessed the women deep in discussion. Though he longed for the comfort of his bed, he forced himself to remain as Julia and his mother talked.

The flickering candlelight threw shadows on the walls, reminding him of the pain now wracking his body. His teaspoon clinked against the rim of the jar as he measured out the amber remedy, and Julia momentarily glanced his way with teary eyes and affirmed his presence with a sad smile.

"Are you all right, William? You look pale."

Perhaps the honey would stay the attack. "I'm okay, thank you."

The warmth of the room offered little comfort as he stirred the honey into his second cup of hot tea. With great effort, he lifted the cup to his lips, the steam rising to settle him. The honeyed concoction provided a brief respite, easing the harsh edges of each breath.

Mother hurled a concerned glance in his direction, her eyes widening as if she had just perceived the reoccurrence of his ailment. She reached over and tenderly pressed her hand against his forehead. "Oh, son!" Her alarm ticked her voice up an octave higher than usual. "You have a fever. You need to be in bed. Rest is what will mend you. Be off with you, dear one." Her soothing voice carried the depth of a mother's concern. "Julia and I make a fine team, just you mind that. We will tend to you and the light as we've done before."

The unwavering determination in her eyes, a maternal resolve that spoke of countless nights spent nursing both wounds and dreams, set him in motion.

He stood, leaning on the table for support. "You're right. I do need to rest. This is the second attack this year, and I'm weary of it."

He glanced at Julia, whose face shone with compassion and concern. She smiled up at him. "I'm sorry you're feeling poorly, William, but your mother's right. We'll take care of everything. Don't worry."

An unconscious sigh sent him into another coughing fit as Julia rose and firmly took his arm. "Please. Let me help you upstairs."

Anything to be near her. He complied, and with a reassuring smile, Julia gently guided him toward the sanctuary of his room. She swung the door open with a creak, pulled back the covers, and began untying his boots.

Caught in the vulnerability of the moment, he shook his head, a self-deprecating frown tugging at his lip as he held back another cough. "I'm so sorry you have to see me like this, an invalid. A weak man once again."

Undeterred by his confession, Julia waved off his concerns with a dismissive flick of her hand. "Stuff and nonsense. A temporary, occasional ailment doesn't mean you're a weak man. It simply means you're human. We all are. And at least you didn't blubber your eyes out like I did in the kitchen just now."

"Oh, Julia, you had good reason to. You have so many life-changing decisions weighing on you. I'm amazed at how strong you are."

Another bout of coughing seized him, so violently that he feared his lungs might burst. Julia fluffed his pillow with a tender touch, and after he slid between the covers, she tucked his blanket snugly around his neck, as if cocooning him in a haven of care.

In the midst of his discomfort, daring questions lingered on the tip of his tongue, ones he feared the answer to. "Will you leave, Gingersnap? Will you marry that rich man, after all?"

Her brow furrowed, her expression a mixture of surprise and determination. "I will not, sir, and you needn't worry about that. I'll be here for the rest of the summer. That you can count on, and we'll see what the future brings. But for now, you need to rest and get well."

Her gentle reassurance hung in the quiet room, offering a momentary respite from her many decisions. But even in this moment, the pain lingered, a constant companion that refused to be cast aside. With each shallow breath, the mustiness of the river pressed against his chest. Pleurisy was a relentless reminder of life's fragility.

In the dimly lit room, Julia lit the lamp and perched on the edge of his bed, hovering over him like a loving mate. A profound realization struck William with the force of the summer storm's lightning.

He'd come to love Julia even more deeply than he had Louise.

A gust of wind rattled the windows, so Julia got up and locked it tight, returning to place a gentle hand on his forehead. "Would you like more tea and honey?"

He nodded. "Thank you. That would be nice."

She left the room, giving him a few moments to ponder and pray. His whispered words mingled with the distant thunder, a plea for divine guidance and a hope for an outcome that transcended the boundaries of mortal understanding. He prayed for strength to weather the storms, both external and internal, and for resilience to face the unknown with unwavering faith.

Love was a beacon in the darkest of storms, a flame that could withstand the howling winds and driving rain.

But what sacrifices might love require of him?

Chapter 14

After a two-week wait, the journey upriver to Rock Island Lighthouse and the prospect of a Sunday dinner with the Diepolders promised the perfect remedy for recovering from recent challenges. Julia's weighty decisions and William's struggle with pleurisy had taken their toll. A respite, it seemed, was much needed for them all.

William had rented the *Sallie Belle*, a thirty-six-foot cabin launch, for their journey. Though much smaller and simpler than Percival's imposing yacht, the well-kept wooden steamer proved just what they needed to take them to Rock Island. He captained the vessel with the skill of a seasoned sailor, tweaking the brass wheel as needed and enjoying lively, light-hearted conversations with Julia and Aunt Dee. A few boats passed by, but on a Sunday morning, the river was pleasantly quiet.

Julia sat with Aunt Dee on maroon velvet cushions just behind the captain's cabin under a roofed deck. They chugged steadily up river, the gentle wind tugging at her bonnet as they approached the lighthouse. She fixed her eyes on the structure, comparing it to the familiar silhouette of Sister's.

Rock Island perched on a rocky shoal in the

narrow passage between Fisher's Landing and Thousand Island Park, where Aunt Emma said she had lived before marrying Uncle Michael. Its brown conical iron tower sat in the middle of the island and rose only about thirty feet, distinctly shorter than Sister Island's taller structure. The keeper's dwelling, a one-and-a-half-story, shingle-style Victorian house, was separate and faced north, surrounded by a concrete seawall, which protected it from the river's harsh conditions. A couple of outbuildings sat on a bigger plot of land than the long, narrow islets that made up Sister's, and it was apparent that many neighbors lived close by. The place had its own charm, its own character.

Yet for Julia, the highlight of coming to Rock Island was not the place but the prospect of seeing her newfound family again—Aunt Emma, Uncle Michael, and even her cousin Ada. Though it had only been three weeks since their initial meeting, she had eagerly awaited this day.

As the steamer docked, the door to the keeper's dwelling swung open, and Aunt Emma, apron-clad, waved joyfully with a warm smile on her face. Her eyes lit up as William, Aunt Dee, and Julia disembarked.

"Welcome to Rock Island! We've been waiting for you." Aunt Emma climbed the steps to the porch. The covered veranda must be a perfect spot for watching ships pass by or reveling in a sunset. "I hope you're hungry. Dinner is almost ready."

Julia smiled at the genuine and warm reception. As they approached, the tantalizing aroma of a home-cooked Sunday dinner greeted them, making Julia's stomach rumble. "I can't wait to see my family again—and more of this place. Is every lighthouse as hospitable as this one and yours?"

"Most are." William squeezed Julia's hand as they approached Aunt Emma.

Her aunt hugged each of them. "You're right on time. I've been cooking up a storm to celebrate your arrival."

Julia held onto her aunt's embrace an extra moment or two, familial warmth filling her heart with joy. "It's so good to see you again, Aunt Emma!"

Their hostess guided them into the parlor where Uncle Michael and another man sat playing checkers. Both men stood as they entered.

Uncle Michael introduced the tall, thin man. "This is Pastor Cantwell from Thousand Island Park. I hope you don't mind him joining us for this family dinner."

William shook his hand. "On the contrary. We're honored. Pleased to meet you, sir."

Uncle Michael motioned toward them. "This is the Sister Island lightkeeper, William Dodge, and his mother, Mrs. Dodge. And this is our niece,

Miss Julia Collins, from Brockville, whom I told you about."

Julia and Aunt Dee curtsied, and Pastor Cantwell acknowledged them with a toothy grin. "Good to know you, folks. Thanks for allowing this old bachelor to crash your party. It isn't often I get a delectable home-cooked meal these days."

Aunt Dee chuckled. "Well, you're welcome to come up to Sister Island anytime, sir. We'd love a visit from a man of the cloth. And our family tradition is much the same as here. The first time, you're company. After that, you're family."

Pastor Cantwell guffawed. "I'll remember that, but it's a far piece up there, isn't it?"

William nodded. "An hour or so by steamer, if you rent or catch a ride on one. Otherwise, it's a few hours by land and a quick skiff ride to the island."

Uncle Michael gestured to the comfortable chairs and invited everyone to make themselves at home. "It's a full day's travel either way, but you'd come home with a contented belly and a light heart. I can guarantee that."

The scent of a hearty stew filled the air, making Julia's mouth water. Aunt Emma brimmed with joy, and so did Julia. She was not alone in the world, after all. She had two families that loved her . . . and she loved them!

The interior of the Diepolder cottage had the

same level of charm as the outside—the worn wooden floors, the crackling cookstove, and the muffled sound of waves crashing against the rocky shore.

As they chatted, Aunt Emma disappeared into the kitchen momentarily, returning with a tray of freshly baked biscuits, which she set on the coffee table. "I thought we could start with these while the stew finishes simmering."

Julia took a biscuit and savored the warm, succulent, buttery goodness. "These are heavenly, Aunt Emma."

Her aunt blushed, clearly pleased with the compliment. "Thank you, niece."

Julia's heart warmed at the moniker, one that spoke of belonging. "But where's Ada?"

"Ada is in Clayton with friends for the weekend. Now, if you'll excuse me, I need to check on the stew." Aunt Emma motioned to Dee. "Can you help, please? We womenfolk need to catch up."

While her aunts addressed the final touches in the kitchen, the conversation between the men flowed effortlessly. Pastor Cantwell shared stories of life in TI Park, as he called it, and Uncle Michael and William regaled them with tales of tending the lighthouses and weathering the storms that swept across the St. Lawrence.

When Aunt Emma called them to dinner, Julia's stomach rumbled in response.

They moved into the dining room and stood around the table.

William's eyes lit up, and he licked his lips. "This looks scrumptious. Thank you for having us."

Aunt Emma chuckled, motioning for them to sit. "I'm glad you all could join us."

As they settled around the table, Aunt Dee glanced around the cottage. "You've made quite a home for yourself, Emma. It's lovely."

"Thank you. Living on Rock Island has its challenges, but there's a particular peace here I cherish." When her aunt spoke of challenges, a flash of concern had crossed her features. What might be the trouble?

Soon a delightful exchange of lighthearted banter filled the room with laughter and cheer. When the meal concluded, Uncle Michael led the men toward the lighthouse for a tour.

While Julia helped the aunts clean up the remnants of the feast, a wistful longing crept over her. She'd like to talk with Aunt Emma alone.

Aunt Dee excused herself to visit the privy, so Julia grabbed the chance to seek Aunt Emma's counsel as they washed and dried the dishes together. "You lived in Brockville most of your life, but then you moved to Thousand Island Park, right? Now you're here on Rock Island. Those were big changes. However did you do it?"

Aunt Emma handed her a bowl to wipe dry

while answering. "You've had to taste a bit of change, already, Julia. But I've found that big changes like living on an island means facing the challenge head on. There are bound to be difficulties, as with any place this side of heaven. But there's also blessing in it—the shared moments of happiness, the way the Thousand Islands community always comes together to help in time of need, and the quiet serenity when the waves lull you to sleep. And best of all, to me, is the love of a good man. What do you plan to do once the summer is over?"

"I'm not sure. Brockville doesn't seem the place for me anymore, but I can't expect the Dodges to keep me forever."

"Well, you're always welcome here, Julia. After all, we're family."

She smiled, appreciating her invitation. "Thank you, but you're still newlyweds, and you wouldn't need me underfoot."

Aunt Emma chuckled. "Ada's here too. And before I forget, just yesterday, I found out that Lucy's daughter—your cousin—was adopted by none other than the Tibbetts Point Lighthouse family in Cape Vincent. She'd be close to your age, I think. It's all quite providential, don't you think?"

Julia gasped. "All three of us live in light-houses? That's so interesting. I'd like to meet her someday."

Aunt Emma nodded. "I haven't met her, either, but you will."

For a moment, they were silent, but Julia dared to go deeper. "How do you make marriage work in such a unique place as a lighthouse on an island?"

Emma's face softened. "Love on an island is like the ebb and flow of the tide. When you love unconditionally and you trust the good Lord to be with you in your journey, it's a bond that can withstand anything. Are you . . . do you have someone special in mind?"

She giggled, her cheeks growing warm. "Perhaps, but that's for a later discussion. There are too many unknowns right now to presume or hope for anything. Can you tell me more about being a keeper's wife? Is it very difficult?"

A complexity of emotions surfaced on her aunt's face, as if she knew what Julia was thinking. "It's an intricate dance between difficulty and reward, as is inherent in any journey of marriage. Being a keeper's wife just adds another layer, and so does step-parenting. Though there may be obstacles littering our path, God can help us. If you haven't read the book of John lately, chapter three might be a good place to start."

She swallowed hard. So her aunt had a similar faith to the Dodges. How curious. "Thanks. I will."

Aunt Emma studied her face as if trying to read

her soul. "When times are tough, the book of truth can help you sort things out. Marriage requires lots of patience, understanding, and a willingness to weather the storms and face the dangers together. But as a keeper's wife, you have to be understanding and ready to work as a team at a moment's notice. Yet, to be honest, the hardest part, for me, is that my bed is empty during the night watch. I'm still getting used to that."

Given her aunt's openness and transparency, maybe in their next conversation Julia could ask about her most pressing matter—faith.

And perhaps one day . . . William.

As William guided the boat back home through the narrow passage between the New York mainland and Wellesley Island, the air carried the musky scent of the river. Mother had fallen asleep where she sat, snoring quietly after the day's excitement.

For several minutes, Julia had been immersed in introspection. Respecting her contemplative state, he chose not to intrude on her thoughts, though he wanted to hear her perspective on the day.

Suddenly, as she observed their surroundings, her eyes brightened. "Please tell me about these islands, William. Until today, I've never been this far up the river."

He swept his hand toward the left, infusing

his voice with the thrill of exploration. "On the port side, Wellesley Island will accompany us for roughly half of our journey. It's one of the grandest islands in the Thousand Islands. Did you know, Gingersnap, that there are more than eighteen hundred islands scattered from Lake Ontario almost to Brockville?"

Julia arched an eyebrow. "Really? I had no idea. Despite having lived along the St. Lawrence my entire life, I never realized the vastness of the islands." Her shoulders slumped, likely from misgivings over missed opportunities.

He tossed her a smile and pointed to the right. "No need for regrets, Gingersnap. You're here now. On the starboard side, feast your eyes on Mandolin Island and Cedar Island. In the distance—that vast expanse of shore is the New York mainland. Look ahead, and you'll spot Frederick Island and then Vanderbilt Island."

Julia shaded her eyes from the sun's brilliance and peered beyond the bow. "As in, *the* Vanderbilts, from the shipping and railroad empire?"

He shrugged. "I can't say for certain. Mother, any insights on that?"

Mother had opened her eyes and pressed a finger to her chin, a thoughtful frown creasing her brow. "Well, goodness. It's quite likely that one of the clan owns it, but you know how they are—keeping things hush-hush. I can't say for sure."

Julia glanced across the panorama of islands that dotted the waterway. The sunlight played upon her hair, shimmering even more beautifully than it did on the gentle waves. He could barely take his eyes off of her. "There are so many. Several smaller than Sister."

"True." He chuckled, turning his attention back to navigating the twists and turns of the waterway and appreciating every minute of captaining this fine vessel. How he wished he owned this steamer instead of the old skiffs at his disposal.

As they glided through the narrowest part of their journey, nestled between rugged shores with lush foliage, the thick scent of pine mingled with the invigorating aroma of the river itself. He slowed to allow them to take it in.

"Just smell the pine, the river, the fresh air. There's nothing like it."

Julia nodded, her eyes sparkling in the sunshine. "Nothing. It's beautiful out here, William."

His mother laughed. "Take it all in, dearie. This is a treat for all of us."

When the expanse of the river widened before them, the mighty St. Lawrence spread out in all its majestic breadth. The sunlight splashed upon the water's surface, casting radiant glitter that shimmered in every ripple and wave.

William waved an arm to his right. "We just passed Comfort Island and Stoney Crest, and Devil's Oven is just ahead."

Julia frowned. "Devil's Oven?"

Mother grinned. "Some say the pirate Bill Johnson hid in the cave on the tiny island while the British were hunting for him during the War of 1812. But I think that's just a tall tale. William's father took me there once, and the cave is much too narrow and would make a poor hiding place."

William grinned at the story he'd heard a dozen times. "Now we're passing Cherry Island on the right, Pullman Island on the left, and up ahead is Alexandria Bay."

Julia smiled. "My parents went to a party on Pullman Island and stayed in Alexandria Bay for several days. They said they met the president, but I can't remember which one. It was just before I was born."

William gasped. "Your parents were at President Grant's reception? They must've been prominent people in your community to be invited."

Julia shrugged. "I guess so."

Suddenly, his mother drew their attention downstream, her enthusiasm bubbling over as she pointed toward the bow. "Look! A saltie is approaching. A beauty, truly. Julia, being near these behemoths is an exhilarating experience, to be sure." She added a gentle warning, her laughter resonating like the ripples from a stone's throw. "*Safely* near, William."

He responded with a chuckle. "Yes, Mother, I'll be careful."

In the distance, a sea-going freighter bore down on them like a colossal titan, its size commanding respect. The hum of its engines resonated through the air, a low and steady vibration almost primal in its power.

As they neared the imposing freighter, Julia's eyes widened, and a potpourri of emotions played across her face. The ship dwarfed their small vessel. She gripped the handrail until her knuckles went white. "I've seen them from Sister Island, but to be in the water with it . . ."

Mother placed a reassuring hand on her shoulder. "Quite a sight, isn't it, dearie? These giants of the sea can be a bit overwhelming, especially when one is beside them in a boat."

"I never imagined they could feel this massive." Julia's voice quivered with a mix of awe and apprehension.

William chimed in with a comforting smile. "No need to worry. These freighters may seem imposing, but they're like gentle giants on the water. See how gracefully they navigate through the river? It's an impressive show of power and precision. You're safe under my command, Gingersnap."

As they came alongside the freighter, the steady thud of its engines became more pronounced, creating a pulsating beat that echoed in his chest. The ship's hull loomed above them, depositing a shadow that momentarily eclipsed the sunlight.

The creaking of the boat beneath them added to the cacophony, and the water, stirred by the freighter's passage, created a gentle swell that rocked their vessel.

As the freighter finally passed, William redirected Julia's attention to their right. "That's Sunken Rock Lighthouse. About a dozen years ago, they replaced the decrepit brick tower with an iron one to better safeguard voyagers and keep them from the dangerous rocks just below the waterline. This river is a challenge to navigate, whether you're in a skiff, a small steamer like this, or a saltie or laker."

As they returned to Sister Island after a magical day of family, fun, and memories, the river reflected the deep blue of the sky.

Julia sighed as if not wanting to leave the boat. "I don't think I can ever go back to life in the city. It's so . . . empty."

William took her hand and helped her onto the deck. "Glad to hear it, my lovely Gingersnap."

Refreshed by the outing, William thanked the good Lord for days like this. And dared to dream of more.

Chapter 15

The next evening, a perfectly clear and still night for her first rowing adventure, Julia climbed into the skiff. The first of many firsts.

She needed to be away from the island. Away from people.

Alone with God.

Thankfully, William had taught her how to row. She could do this.

Her nerves fired as she settled onto the weathered wooden seat, the skiff rocking gently under her. The air brushed against her face, carrying whispers of comfort. Stretching before her, the river created a vast spectacle of heavenly twilight sparkling on the tips of the gentle waves.

She sat a moment, contemplating the significance of her upcoming decision. She'd contemplated it for weeks, and now she'd settle it. Yes, she still marveled at nature's wonder, but now she had to acknowledge the Creator God of it all. He had always seemed so far beyond her reach, and yet, maybe she'd just ignored Him. Until now.

He had been there all the time. From the twinkling stars to the cricket's call. In the lap of the waves on the shore and the distant thunder. In the rustle of the leaves in an old oak tree and in the sleeping flowers beneath it. Even in the changing seasons, God sketched a picture of His invitation to grow. To trust. To rest in Him. To become new.

All of creation shouted of the Creator—of her Creator—the universe declaring His power, His love, His mercy, whether or not she had wanted to acknowledge it.

Now, the question was—would she, could she join creation in that declaration?

She dug the oars into the water, slowly maneuvering out from the dock. She'd skirt the island, staying close enough to be safe. Until she met Him.

Truth was, the whispers of His love had grown indistinct in the aftermath of her parents' deaths. She hadn't felt His comforting touch, heard His guiding voice, or engaged in conversation with Him for a long, long time. In that deep void left by grief, she chose her own compass, leaning heavily on the teachings of her father to construct a world that felt secure. Yet, in doing so, she had distanced herself from the very Creator who had shaped all she held dear.

Instead of entrusting her life to the Creator, she shaped her reality through the narrow lens of finite understanding. Her father's philosophy became her safeguard, but it also obscured the true infinite treasures and wisdom that Scripture had so recently unveiled.

With each stroke, the oars sliced through the water, propelling her from the familiar shores.

The island, with its memories of so many spiritual conversations, hours of Scripture reading, and hard-fought battles of the soul, remained a safe distance away.

Gratitude welled up as she remembered William's patient teachings, the moments when he guided her hands on the worn wooden oars, imparting the wisdom of the river.

The skiff danced on the water as she rounded the island, carrying her toward the main channel. She needed this isolation. Craved the embrace of the vast expanse that impersonated the depths of her own soul.

With every stroke and with whispered prayers for guidance, she unraveled the tangled threads of years of confusion. The sky transformed into a tapestry of stars, a celestial scene under which she could pour out her heart. She spoke of dreams shattered, of hopes deferred, and of the ache that nestled in the chambers of her chest.

Though she stayed within sight of Sister and paddled against the current to stay in one spot, the rhythmic lullaby of the oars became a cadence for her confession. In the solitude, she surrendered the fragments of her life, like scattered seashells along the shore. The weight lifted, replaced by a raw vulnerability under the watchful rising moon.

Having memorized Psalm 19 for this moment, she lifted her voice in confession. " 'The heavens declare the glory of God; and the firmament sheweth his handywork. Day unto day uttereth speech, and night unto night sheweth knowledge. There is no speech nor language, where their voice is not heard.' Lord! I see now that nature proclaims the creative power and majesty of You, and it shouts that You are always here. With me. Even when I felt so far from You, You were there with me all the time."

When she was eight and spent the summer with her granny, she had given her life to Him, but not fully, not like He wanted her to. Though she never really doubted there was a God, she'd ignored Him. Avoided Him because of her mother and the pain of her losses.

But now He beckoned her back into His arms, as if He yearned for her. Ached for her. Wanted her. Tugging her close so she could hear Him again.

Whispering love. Murmuring healing. Imparting faith. Flooding her with hope.

And belonging.

With each breath, memories flooded back—childhood innocence, the comforting embrace of her granny, and the distant echoes of faith that had once resonated in her soul. She knelt in the skiff, her fingers tracing the grooves in the weathered wood.

Tears welled in her eyes as she closed them. Memories of her mother's harshness, of loss and heartache, mingled with the memories of a summer long ago. The compassion of God's love, once familiar, was drowned out by the cacophony of life's struggles.

But today was different. Tonight, the world exhaled a divine breath, wrapping her in an embrace she had long resisted. The flickering stars winked welcome, and Julia sensed His presence, a yearning that transcended the barriers she had erected.

In the stillness, she whispered words long held captive within her soul. "I'm sorry," she said, her voice barely audible. "I've avoided You for so long, blamed You for the pain, for the losses. I'm so sorry."

As if responding to her confession, a gentle puff of wind swept through her hair, stirring the surrounding air. Julia's tears fell freely, a cascade of surrender and repentance. She bowed her head, aching for the love she had pushed away to envelop her.

As the skiff bobbed through the inky waters, her own emotions ebbed and flowed with it. The salt on her cheeks mingled with the cool night air, and in communion with God, she found peace.

The skiff, now adrift on the current, became a vessel for her rebirth. With every whispered prayer, she released the burdens that anchored her to the past and set sail into the unknown waters of a new dawn.

"I'm Yours, Lord." She raised her arms to the

heavens, her words a fragile offering. "Take my stubborn ways, my rebellious heart. Take my faithless past, my pain, my heartache."

A profound peace settled over her, as if the weight she had carried for so long had finally lifted. The river resonated with His divine presence, embracing her in a love that surpassed her understanding. In that sacred moment of surrender, Julia's soul reunited with its Creator.

She was His.

She opened her eyes to the moon's illumination, like a symbol of her rekindled faith. With a heart unburdened, she rose from her knees and sat on the bench with a light heart. Julia had found a home in the arms of the God who had waited patiently for her return.

As if she were awakening from a cold, hard winter, tears flooded her eyes. Ran down her cheeks. Her heart fairly burst with revelation.

She was not alone. She would never be alone. He was the God of love. The God who cared. He—the Father, Son, and Spirit—was her family.

Her home.

She recalled her granny's favorite hymn, a song she knew well. With new-found faith, she wiped her tears and sang out her favorite childhood hymn loud and free.

All things bright and beautiful
All creatures great and small

All things wise and wonderful
The Lord God that made them all

Each little flower that opens
Each little bird that sings
He made their glowing colors
And made their tiny wings
The purple headed mountains
The rivers running by
The sunset and the morning
That brightens up the sky

He gave us eyes to see them
And lips that we might tell
How great is the Almighty
Who has made all things well

The evening air seemed to bear the weight of William's concern as he ascended the ladder. With each step, his prayers for Julia mingled with the hum of the lighthouse.

Earlier that evening, an unease had settled over the cottage as Julia withdrew into a mysterious silence. She had forgone dinner, leaving an empty chair at the table, and retired to her bedroom without a word. William's worry had grown, prompting him to pray for her while he went about the familiar routine of tending to the lighthouse.

Now, as he lit the lamp, a haunting melody reached his ears—an ethereal voice that danced on the water. Startled, he hurried out onto the parapet and strained his senses, seeking the source. Julia's voice, sweet and steadfast, reached him, but its origin remained elusive. The melody beckoned him to search the far reaches of the island, and with binoculars in hand, he scanned the soon-coming darkness.

She wasn't on the porch or in the cottage or on the island, far as he could see. A sense of urgency gripped him as the sweep of the lighthouse beam illuminated an empty dock, void of the skiff that was usually moored and at the ready. Panic set in as he waited for the light to pass again, hoping to catch a glimpse of Julia.

Frantically, he peered into the distance. Why would she venture into the dark and dangerous waters at night?

The haunting strains of "All Creatures Great and Small" echoed in the night, adding an eerie layer to the mystery. He honed in on the direction of her voice and gasped.

As the realization hit him, he cupped his hands and shouted into the murkiness. "Julia? Is that you out on the river in the dark?"

The light illuminated Julia in the skiff, out in the middle of the main channel! She waved both hands, but then the beam of the lighthouse unveiled a looming danger—a massive laker heading directly toward her.

Fear tightened its grip. He called out again,

urgency lacing his voice. "Julia! There's a laker coming your way. Hurry to shore! It's not safe out there!"

He scrambled down the ladder and raced to enlist his mother's help. "Mother!" His voice pierced the quiet night. "Julia's in trouble. Come quick."

William ran to the water's edge and raised his lamp high. He watched helplessly as Julia strained at the oars, the small boat battling against the waves. The ominous silhouette of the laker loomed closer, a deadly threat in the moonlit night.

As the moments ticked slowly by and Julia came closer and closer to the island, away from the ship, his mother joined him, a blanket in hand. "What is she doing out there at this hour, son?"

He shrugged, raising his palms to the sky, his eyes never leaving Julia's frantic struggle. "Lord only knows, but that laker would've toppled her over had I not warned her."

Julia finally reached the shore nearest them, just as the laker passed by the island. William rushed into the river, the chilly water soaking his slacks and boots as he helped her out of the boat and guided her onto the shore.

Mother approached and wrapped a woolen blanket around Julia's shoulders, kissing her on the cheek while scolding her gently. "You could have perished out there, dearie."

Relief mixed with concern as they stood on

the shore, the calm and serene of the night having transformed into a harrowing ordeal, reminding him of the unpredictable nature of the St. Lawrence and the fragility of those who dared challenge it.

He put his arms around Julia and hugged her. "Let's get you inside, Gingersnap."

The cottage, bathed in the glimmer of lamplight, welcomed them as they returned from the shore. Mother busied herself in the kitchen, having promised them something hot to eat and drink, fixing tea and before long, placing the leftovers from dinner on the table. The aroma of vegetable soup filled the air, a comforting contrast to the tension that lingered.

They settled around the table, William across from Julia, the flickering flames of the candles casting dancing shadows. Mother poured tea into delicate cups, her eyes searching Julia's face for an explanation. His work as the lightkeeper could wait—her confession, he sensed, was much more important.

Julia took a sip of her tea before finally breaking the silence. "When we visited Aunt Emma, she suggested I read the book of John chapter three, so I did. I realized that the spiritual birth in the text was a choice I needed to make. I didn't choose my parents or many of the challenges I've faced so far, but I could make the most important choice of my life."

The revelation produced a profound shift in the atmosphere. Mother set her teacup down, her eyes softening with understanding, while William endeavored to absorb the import of what she was saying. A giant lump formed in his throat, and tears threatened at the back of his eyelids. He blinked them back.

Could it be?

Julia traced her finger along the rim of her teacup. "My time here has been a journey of confusion, curiosity, conviction, confession, and now conversion. Just as my granny had hoped, I suspect. You two have been the embodiment of the peace, joy, and love that I've longed for, and tonight I made the decision to give my heart to the Lord. That's what I was doing out there on the river."

William let out a gusty breath. All the talks, all the prayers—they had borne fruit! "Oh, Julia! This is the best news I've heard in . . . forever!" His voice cracked under the emotion of it, but he didn't care. She was His, and now William could hope that, one day, she could be *his* as well.

Mother's eyes shone with a brew of emotions—understanding, pride, and a touch of relief. "Julia, my dearest girl, that's a profound choice you've made. It changes everything for you. For eternity."

William could hardly contain the smile that blazed across his face. "My precious Gingersnap,

I'm thrilled that you've joined us in a common faith. It makes all the difference for your future."

He yearned to say *for our future* yet restrained that sentiment, at least for the moment. Undoubtedly, her decision could significantly impact the foundation of their relationship, should she decide to embrace it.

Julia returned the smile, gratitude shining in her eyes. "Thank you both. Your love and support means more than words can express. I've been wrestling with this for a while, and tonight, everything fell into place."

Mother nodded, her hands folding around her teacup. "Sometimes, the river of life takes unexpected turns. I'm glad you found your way to shore. And speaking of rivers, why don't you tell us more about your time out there tonight?"

Julia's eyes illuminated with joy and newfound peace. "It was a moment of surrender, really. I felt a connection to someone greater than myself. Being on that river felt like a symbolic journey. The water, the moonlight—it was all a part of something divine. I wanted to embrace it fully, knowing I had made the most important choice of my life. I gave my life to God, and now, I think the real voyage is about to unfold."

The wonder of Julia's words settled in their midst, a sacred moment shared among the small circle, punctuated by the crackling of the cookstove.

He reached across the table, placing a comforting hand on Julia's. Then he excused himself, a subtle smile playing on his lips. "If you'll excuse me, duty calls, ladies. Sleep well, and I'll see you in the morning."

As he climbed the stairs, his thoughts thundered in the tower's solitude. The revelation of Julia's transformation ignited his heart, yet a different intensity flickered within—the realization that his love for her might actually bear fruit. It was a truth he had carefully guarded, knowing that their distinctly different views of faith would never create a firm foundation for a future together.

But tonight, everything was different. The very thing that had been a wedge between them, the source of unspoken tension, was now what united them. The future, once murky with impossibilities, shimmered with the potential for a shared journey—a journey that might bridge the gap between their souls and the faith that had once seemed an insurmountable divide.

Was there a future predestined for the two of them? Did Julia feel the same pull, the same shift in the currents of their lives? What was God up to?

He stared into the vast expanse surrounding the lighthouse and surrendered to the unknown. As long as the good Lord was in charge, it would be all right.

Chapter 16

The late-afternoon sun scattered a cheery golden cloak over Sister Island, and a splash of colors stretched to the horizon. Waves crashed onto the rocks below. The breeze carried the scent of the river. Just three days since Julia met the Creator, and everything was different. Alive. Real.

Inspired by the enchantment and serenity of the moment, she shifted on the stool William had brought up to the parapet for her so she could paint from an eagle's eye view. She dipped her brush into the yellow on her palette. William stood against the railing of the lighthouse tower, seemingly lost in thought, framed by the breathtaking view of the St. Lawrence River.

Her heart swelled with gratitude for the man who had become a beacon of faith, hope, and love in her life. As she sketched his image, the river shimmered with reflections of the sun's slowly fading rays, splashing a cordial radiance over the landscape. The silhouettes of distant shores added layers to the horizon, creating a perspective that appeared to stretch into eternity.

"I love this place," she whispered, her words carried away by a rush of air. "I never want to leave."

He turned to her. "It's a special place, indeed. The tranquility of Sister Island is like a salve for the soul."

"And so are you." Her confession declared the depth of her emotions. "You've been my lighthouse, William, guiding me through the storms and illuminating the path to serenity."

His eyes flashed surprise, and he stood straighter. "Thank you, Gingersnap. That means a lot."

"Stay right there, please, and let me add the lightkeeper to my canvas before the light fades."

He tipped his head a degree or two to the side, puffing out his chest. "Like this?"

She nodded. "Perfect."

As she captured the essence of the moment with her pencil and brush, her heart pounded. Did he feel the same as she? She had considered it for the last three days, and the strokes of her brush mirrored the emotions swirling within her—admiration, affection, and a yearning for something more.

William remained still, immersed in the allure of the landscape, while Julia's artistic endeavor became an expression of her love for him. The wind tousled his hair, and the sunlight highlighted the contours of his profile. The way he stood, his silhouette against the tranquil river, was a symbol of the strength and comfort he had provided her in the past months. His frame against the expansive river embodied the spirit of the lightkeeper—a rugged and resilient presence in the face of the ever-changing currents.

But as the canvas transformed into a representation of the scene before her, her heart ached with uncertainty. What if he didn't share the same depth of feelings? What if their connection was merely friendship and nothing more than a figment of her imagination?

After an hour or more, William stretched and sauntered over. "It's a beautiful time to capture the river. May I see?"

"Of course. I hope you don't mind that I ignored the river and focused on the keeper instead."

He observed her work with a tilt of his head, as if silently asking questions. "You're a gifted artist, Gingersnap. Truly."

"You think? Thank you. I still have a lot to learn."

Julia assessed her own work with a sigh of satisfaction—and a twinge of vulnerability. The image of the island's guardian had emerged on the page, a blaze of life. The movement of light and shadow, the details etched with care, brought a sense of vitality to the portrait. Julia's eyes flicked between the image and the man himself, gauging his reaction.

William licked his lips, his gaze lingering on the composition. "You see me this way?"

She dipped her chin. "I do, William. But there's so much more I'd like to capture before the sun sets. Please, let me finish."

He nodded, returning to the spot where he had stood against the parapet, the sun projecting long shadows around him. Tension hung in the air, and Julia couldn't help but wonder if he approved of her work or if something in her depiction didn't align with his self-perception.

She continued to paint, each stroke a labor of love and admiration for the man before her. The colors on the painting wove a narrative of the connection they shared, the unspoken bond that had grown amidst the charm of Sister Island.

As the sun dipped lower on the horizon, a dazzling cascade of colors washed over the scene, and her brush moved with a sense of urgency. She wanted to capture every nuance, every detail that made William the unique and inspiring presence he was in her life.

Finally, as she put the finishing touches on the composition, she stepped back, analyzing the canvas and the man before her. "There." Both passion and nervousness crept into her voice. "What do you think?"

He turned his attention to the portrait, and a thoughtful expression crossed his face. "It's . . . it's incredible. You've captured something beyond the surface. It's as if you've painted . . . my soul."

The tension dissolved, replaced by a shared understanding of the connection they had forged. She smiled, grateful that her labor of love had been met with his approval.

"I think that sometimes, the best way for me to express the beauty of a moment is through art, and it's not just the island or the river that are so alluring. You, William, are a part of the timeless appeal that defines Sister Island. And now, my life."

William took her hand and kissed the back of it. "You have brought grace and heavenly hope to this place, and into my life, Julia. Neither the island nor I will ever be the same."

The sun dipped below the horizon, and the splendor of the sunset washed over the lighthouse tower. She stood with him, admiring the piece of art that would forever hold the essence of that tranquil and spectacular moment on the St. Lawrence, suspended by the strokes of her brush.

The colors of the sky deepened into shades of orange and pink, sparkling on the water in a dazzling display. She took a deep breath, inhaling the pure, invigorating air. Her mind flew to the possibilities of what might be, and her heart clenched with trepidation of what might not. Yet a deep sense of awe and gratitude took over as she delighted in God's wonderful creation before her.

William broke the silence with a whisper. "It's time to light the lamp, but I still have much to say. Wait here, please."

She nodded, continuing to soak in the sights around her. The magic of twilight added to the majesty of the scene. Birds flitted overhead, soaring gracefully against the radiant sky.

What did he want to say to her that he could barely whisper his request?

The illumination of the lighthouse lamp bathed the tower in a cheerful, flickering light as William returned, his silhouette strong against the evening sky. As he approached, a smile lifted the corners of his mouth and created creases at the corners of his eyes, his long, dark lashes framing them handsomely. The air between them seemed charged with an unspoken anticipation, like lightning before it strikes. The twilight hues deepened, projecting a magical spell over the landscape.

He took her hands in his and swallowed, his face somber. "I have a confession to make. Ever since I first saw you at your grandmother's funeral, I've dreamed of you. When you came to the island, I feared you."

She blinked. "Feared me?"

He nodded but didn't explain. "These past months with you have been like creating a grand masterpiece together." His voice carried both sincerity and vulnerability. "You've been my joy, Julia, and you have created a world of vibrant colors with hope for a bright and glorious future. Truth is, I've come to love you more than I ever thought possible. Might you . . . do you feel the same way?"

His words floated between them, and Julia's heart skipped a beat. She saw her own feelings in the depth of his eyes.

A wave of emotion surged through her as she took in the reality of his confession. "As you can see by this portrait I just created, William, you've become my inspiration and my muse. I love you, too, more than I could have imagined."

Their hands found each other in the fading light, fingers intertwining in a hushed promise. The world around them faded away, leaving only the two of them illuminated by the comfort of the lighthouse lamp.

As the birds continued their graceful soaring in the sky and the waves whispered tales of endless possibilities, they stood together, their hearts entwined in a celebration of love that transcended the colors of twilight and embraced the promise of a future infused with shades of shared dreams and mutual love.

Caught in a whirlwind of emotions, William struggled to convey the immense ecstasy and gratitude swirling inside him as he admired Julia, so radiant, so captivating in the moonlight.

"You're enchanting. Do you know that?"

He took her hand and hoped his fumbling words would caress her, as gentle as a butterfly's wings—but still they failed to capture the depth of his feelings.

Julia's breath caught audibly in her throat, her face expressing surprise at the compliment. "No one has ever said that to me."

William struggled to discern her reaction during the long pause, a moment of unspoken uncertainty. Was she vexed or pleased by his words? But he discerned the importance of his statement and the rarity of such compliments in her life. "I'm only speaking what my heart sees."

Her fingers brushed against his, a fleeting touch that sent a shiver down his spine. It was as if they had touched the edge of a flame—a connection that ignited something within them both. Her lemon verbena scent wafted in the air as her eyes widened. She withdrew her hand, plunging it into her pocket as if seeking refuge from the unexpected spark.

Confusion and yearning battled within him. He took a step closer, wanting to bridge the gap that had momentarily widened between them. "Julia, I didn't mean to make you uncomfortable. I just wanted you to know what I see when I look at you."

She met his gaze, and a subtle shift occurred. Her expression softened, and a hint of a smile awakened on her lips. Julia leaned her head on his arm and sighed. "Thank you, William. I've just never felt so cherished. You and your mother have accepted me, loved me, cared for me more than my family ever did. And certainly, more than my friends and acquaintances."

He took her in his arms and held her tight, kissing the top of her head. "I'm so sorry for the pain you've gone through, my darling. I wish I could heal every broken part of your past. But we know who can, don't we?"

Julia looked up at him and smiled. "We do. I've never felt so free as I have these past few days. Free from the hurt, the grief, the emptiness. The memory of it all is still there, but no longer surrounded by pain. How can that be? God really does work miracles of the heart, doesn't He?"

"That's our God, Julia." The depth of her understanding surprised him. He tightened his embrace, grateful for the shared faith that had brought them both healing. She now truly was a like-minded believer who added a sense of completeness to his life.

As William stood there, his heart pounding like a drum in his chest, he found himself drawn inexorably closer to her. Her eyes, pools of liquid amber, held him captive, their intensity pulling him into a realm of profound hope.

The air around them seemed to hum with anticipation, charged with an undeniable electricity that bound them together. He could feel the warmth of her breath mingling with his, a tantalizing dance that stirred something deep within him.

"You're an intricate part of our lives here, Julia." His admission tumbled in his gut.

As he looked into her eyes, all his fears melted away, leaving only the raw, unbridled longing that pulsed through his veins. But despite the overwhelming urge to bridge the distance between them, doubt and fear gnawed at the edges of his consciousness, threatening to extinguish the fragile flame of desire.

Was it the right time to kiss her? Oh, how he wanted to!

Julia's bottom lip trembled, just a little, and he hesitated. Was she afraid?

Without being sure she was ready, he couldn't bring himself to take that step. Instead, he kissed the top of her head and looked down at her with knit brows. "You said you never want to leave here, but could you really see yourself living here on the island, Julia? Might this be your future? Your calling?"

Julia sucked in a breath, and a smile bloomed on her lips. "Yes, William. I could." Conviction strengthened her voice. "But I still have so many unknowns. So many decisions to make."

His pulse quickened, and a thin sheen of perspiration dampened his brow. He swiped it away, nervous energy coursing through him. "Are you still considering Percival's proposal?"

Julia threw back her head and guffawed, the sound resounding in the quiet of the evening.

"Absolutely not! Actually, I haven't thought of him since he left. But I guess I should write him a letter and decline officially so he doesn't appear on our shores as he threatened."

He huffed his relief and then winked. "I'm so happy to hear that, Gingersnap."

She giggled and rolled her eyes. "The unknowns and decisions I was alluding to are all the details of dealing with Granny's estate. Her house. Her belongings. Even her debts, I expect. When she died, the solicitor told me I couldn't live in the house and that I had to come here for the summer to fulfill her wishes. Then he said that come September, I would assume full responsibility of everything once I meet with him."

"That is a lot of responsibility. Is there much to deal with?"

She shrugged, her gaze fixed on the horizon. "I honestly don't know. The solicitor wouldn't discuss anything with me until I spent the summer here."

The seriousness of such matters temporarily overshadowed the thrill and amazement of the acknowledgement of their love. He'd have to be patient—and supportive. "Would you ever want to go back and live in your granny's home, if that were an option?"

Julia shook her head, a wistful expression crossing her face. "Too many memories. When I first came here, I couldn't wait for the summer to end and get back to the city. But now? I can't imagine going back there. Not without Granny. Not without . . ." Her gaze darted to him and she looked away. "And I don't belong in Brockville anymore either."

He blew out a ragged breath, comforted by her words. "Well then, we'll have to trust the Lord with all of the details. He will guide you in all the decisions you'll have to make, I'm sure of it. I'll help, if you'd like. Mother too."

She turned to him, gratitude shining in her eyes. "Thank you, William. Your support means more to me than you can imagine. It's daunting, facing the unknown, but with you and your mother by my side, I feel a sense of peace."

He reached for her hand, giving it a reassuring squeeze. "We're in this together, Julia. You are not alone. You'll never be alone. Whatever comes, we'll face it as a team. And with the Lord guiding us, I believe we'll find the right path."

She tipped her chin up. "Wherever God leads, it'll be the best path of all, and I'm ready to follow."

Chapter 17

Before the first light of dawn, Julia perched at the tiny desk in her room, prepared to pen a letter to Percival in which she would officially decline his proposal. She had no intention of seeing him again and had to make that known. The soft light of the pre-dawn cloaked the room, the flickering candle prodding her to write, the quiet of the morning lending peace for the task at hand.

With a steadying breath, she grasped the pen, feeling the cool smoothness against her fingertips. The fine linen paper beneath awaited the words that would order the course of her future. As ink met paper, Julia's thoughts flowed, each stroke of the pen an earnest attempt to articulate the complexities of her thoughts.

The creak of the floorboards outside her door and the distant chirping of waking birds served as comfort to her contemplation. Percival and his family would be negatively affected by her words, and with their power in the community, might possibly retaliate against her slight. But she delved into the reasons, weaving phrases that conveyed respect for the family and the person Percival was, yet also delicately unveiling the divergence of their paths.

As the sunrise splashed the sky with the pink

and gold of morning, Julia reread the letter. Inevitably, Percival and his parents would disapprove of her decision and be angry with her, but with a prayer for peace, a strange calm settled over her. A deep sigh escaped her, releasing the worry that had been rising within her.

She'd trust God with all of it. Suddenly, a newfound strength surged within her. If needed, she would weather the storm of their wrath and hope to emerge unscathed, shielded by a prayer from the vindictiveness that was a part of their characters.

With a final stroke of the pen, Julia set the letter down and leaned back in her chair, contemplating the sunrise outside her window, knowing that the courses of two lives had just taken life-altering turns with the strokes of her pen.

As she blew out the candle, ready to face the consequences of her decision, she couldn't help but feel a sense of liberation. In rejecting Percival, she was also freeing herself from the shadows of her past, leaving her unfettered to embrace the future that awaited her.

A gentle knock on Julia's door jolted her from her thoughts. Aunt Dee's familiar voice followed. "May I come in, dearie?"

Julia rose. What could she want? "Of course, you may."

Aunt Dee eased the creaking door open, poking her head around before stepping inside.

Julia smiled. "Good morning. Am I late for breakfast?"

"No, no. Good morning. Julia. I wanted to give you this." She extended a thick manila envelope toward her. It bore the address of Granny's solicitor. "The mail boat just arrived a few minutes ago. The postman is having a cup of coffee with William before he leaves."

Julia gasped, setting the envelope on the desk, grabbing her newly written letter, and waving it in the air. "How fortuitous! I just finished my letter to Percival. Do you have an envelope I could use, please?"

Aunt Dee blinked, a grin gracing her lips. "Well, that is providential. Our postal man only comes by every week or two. Sometimes three. And yes, I have an envelope. Come, dearie, let's get it in the mail before Mr. Ellis scurries off."

Julia followed her downstairs, the wooden steps groaning beneath their footsteps. Aunt Dee retrieved an envelope from a drawer and handed it to her, and she hastily addressed it. With the sealed letter in hand, they entered the kitchen where the postman chatted about his latest fishing exploits with William.

Mr. Ellis glanced up as Julia entered, a genial smile on his weathered face. She handed him the letter, and he read the address. "Brockville, Canada, eh? Well, now, little lady. I'll have this on its way today, and I hope you find the missive I delivered brings you good news."

She bobbed a curtsy. "Thank you, sir. And I hope your day of deliveries will be pleasant."

Her decision was now sealed within the envelope, soon to be on its way.

As the postman bid his farewell, Aunt Dee set out breakfast, but Julia found herself merely pushing the oats around in her bowl. Her weighty thoughts lingered upstairs, sealed within a manila envelope.

At length, Aunt Dee gently intervened. "My dear girl, go on up and get that letter, if you'd like. I see you'll not eat a thing until you do."

William concurred with a smile. "Go on, then, Gingersnap. Let's see what it has to say."

"Thank you. I'm ever so nervous about it." She excused herself from the table, ran up the stairs, retrieved the envelope, and returned to the kitchen. "It's from Granny's solicitor."

Aunt Dee nodded knowingly, exchanging Julia's now-cold tea for a freshly poured cup. "I suspected as much. Drink your tea while it's still hot and take a few bites of your oatmeal. Then we'll deal with your letter together."

She set the missive on her lap and followed Aunt Dee's advice, eating a few spoonfuls of oatmeal and sipping the tea. Yet her mind remained fixed on the impending revelation within the envelope.

Unable to endure the suspense any longer, she grabbed the sealed envelope and thrust it toward William. "You open it and read it to us, please. I'm too nervous."

He nodded, setting aside his spoon and carefully opening the manila envelope. Inside was a green velvet box and a letter. He handed the box to her. "Open it, darling."

She did and giggled, her face lighting up with a joy that rivaled the sunrise. "Grandma's pearls! The solicitor had them all the time."

Aunt Dee stood and clasped them around Julia's neck while tears of joy rolled down her cheeks. "They're beautiful, dearie. I remember your grandmother wearing them with pride. Said they were her mother's."

She touched them gingerly. "They were. Of all the beautiful, costly things Granny owned, this was the one thing I had hoped to have. And now, I do!"

William chuckled. "They're lovely on you, Julia. And now, the letter."

Aunt Dee sat and resumed eating her breakfast while Julia nervously watched William peruse the letter. After what seemed like ages, he cleared his throat before reading aloud.

"Dear Julia,
    I hope this letter finds you well, and I am pleased to know you have spent the

better part of your summer at Sister Island Lighthouse with your grandmother's friend, Mrs. Dodge, as requested.

While you've sojourned there, I've been working on your grandmother's estate, and I now regret to be the bearer of somber news regarding your grandmother's legacy. As the executor of the will, it is my responsibility to inform you of the current state of affairs.

After settling all outstanding debts, including the necessary death taxes, I must convey that the remaining assets of the estate are not as substantial as one might hope. Unfortunately, the financial situation leaves little choice but to sell the house and its contents to cover the remaining expenses.

I have enclosed the pearls your grandmother insisted you have above all else. I hope they will be a comfort to you.

I understand the sentimental value that your grandmother's property holds for you, and it pains me to deliver this message. The proceeds of the sale will settle the remaining financial obligations, leaving only a modest amount that we will disburse to you as the sole beneficiary.

I am here to provide any assistance or clarification you may require throughout this process. Please do not hesitate to reach out with questions or concerns.

Wishing you strength and understanding during this challenging time.

Sincerely,

Mr. Stanley McTavish, Solicitor"

A heavy silence settled over the kitchen, the reality of Mr. McTavish's words hanging in the air like a shroud. Julia, her hands trembling, looked to Aunt Dee and William for support as the reality of the situation sank in.

Aunt Dee reached out, grasping her hand. "It'll be okay, dearie. I believe your grandmother knew you needed us to be your family, and that we are. Always. You needn't worry about where you will live or how you will survive, for you have a place here in our home and in our hearts. Just you mind that."

William took her other hand in his. "Mother is right, Julia. You are family."

Julia looked at them, tears streaming down her cheeks, gratitude and confusion mingling in her thoughts. While William had confessed his love for her, he hadn't proposed, and the uncertainty of his meaning nagged at her. Was his love familial, akin to a brother and sister, or did it hold the depth of a romantic relationship she yearned for?

Her mind swirled with conflicting emotions,

and the revelation of the dwindling inheritance only added to the chaos. Her parents were gone, Granny was gone, and now a significant part of her legacy was slipping away. What was she to do?

She needed time alone to evaluate the whirl-wind of thoughts. "Thank you, Aunt Dee, William. I appreciate your support. Please excuse me."

She retreated to her room, the creak of the door closing behind her imitating the closing chapter of her past. Sitting at the desk, she stared at the letter in her hands, the words blurring through a veil of tears. Julia pulled out her handkerchief as she grappled with the myriad of emotions that surged within her.

As she considered the next steps on this unexpected journey, she yearned for clarity and a sense of purpose. The room, once a haven, now felt like a chamber of uncharted tomorrows, and she faced the daunting task of navigating the uncertain path that lay ahead.

But in that moment, she remembered who could help. She bent her head and prayed, giving her cares to God and asking for peace and hope for her future.

The soft crunch of gravel beneath William's boots resounded through the grounds of Sister Island as he paced, his mind a tumultuous whirl-wind of worry and prayer for Julia's future—for their future. The day had unfolded with Julia sequestered in her room, a veil of sorrowful contemplation shrouding her. Though every fiber of his being yearned to offer comfort, he sensed that she needed the solitude to navigate the labyrinth of her thoughts.

Finally, as dusk settled in, Julia emerged from her room, her countenance carrying a newfound peace—a sight for which he had fervently prayed. The lines of tension that had etched her face earlier had softened, replaced by a serene resolve that hinted at a battle fought and won.

As they gathered around the dinner table, the scent of his mother's pan-fried fish and the vibrant tanginess of pickled beets filled their senses. As they ate, Julia shared about her day, her words carrying both introspection and resolution.

"Today has been life-changing for me." Julia's eyes met his with a depth of tranquility that spoke volumes. "As you know, I wrote the letter to Percival, carefully declining his proposal, and I'm glad that is done. And I've been thinking through the solicitor's letter."

He held his breath as Julia continued, recounting the challenges of grappling with Granny's inheritance—or the lack thereof.

"As I prayed, I realized that Granny's legacy is not solely defined by material possessions. It's the memories, the love, and the strength she imparted to me. That, in itself, is an inheritance beyond measure."

His mother sighed. "Oh, my girl, you've embraced a truth that will undergird you all your life."

William's admiration for Julia's resilience and the wisdom she had gained through her newfound faith only deepened. His heart filled with hope. She was a woman of character, indeed.

With dinner done and the kitchen clean, he took the wet dish towel from Julia's hand. "Join me in the lighthouse, will you, Gingersnap?"

"Okay . . ." She shot his mother a questioning look.

Mother grinned widely, a flicker of amusement betraying that she had foreknowledge of his request—and possibly his plans. "Go ahead, dearie. I have sewing to do, and then I'm going to bed. It's been a long day for all of us."

William kissed his mother goodnight, and Julia hugged her before they climbed the stairs to the lamp room together. After he lit the lamp and checked that everything was as it should be, he joined her on the parapet.

A crisp wind swept across Sister Island, carrying the scent of the river and the distant promise of the future. The panoramic view of the St. Lawrence stretched before them like a masterpiece graced with the allure of the setting sun.

Like God's fresh mercies in the morning, sunsets never grew old.

As they surveyed the mesmerizing scene together, a comfortable silence enveloped them. William couldn't help but steal glances at Julia, captivated by the way the fading sunlight illuminated her features, creating a radiant glimmer around her and making her silky hair shimmer, her face as peaceful as an angel's.

Unable to contain his feelings any longer, he gently took her hand. She shivered at his touch. "Julia, these moments with you are like heaven written on my heart. I can't imagine my life without you by my side."

Their hands intertwined, and the cool breath of the summer's evening played with Julia's hair. He swept a few strands from her face, her eyes dancing with anticipation.

He reached for her other hand, holding both as if they were delicate treasures. "From the moment we met, I knew there was something extraordinary about you. Today, under the tower of this lighthouse, I want to ask you something." He took a deep breath, his gaze unwavering. "Julia, will you make me the happiest man alive and be my partner in this grand adventure called life?"

The question lingered in the silence, carrying with it the weight of their shared moments, joy-filled laughter, and the unspoken connection that had grown between them.

Her features brimmed with emotion as she searched his face. With a luminous smile, she whispered, "You said that we are family, and I'd love for that to be official. Yes, William. A thousand times, yes."

With tender care, he caressed her face, locking eyes with her in sheer amazement. Gone was the quivering lip and fearful gaze. She was ready.

Slowly, he stepped closer, softly brushing his lips against hers. When her eyes fluttered shut in response, he leaned in once more to savor another kiss.

As their lips met in a delicious and lingering kiss, a cascade of sensations enveloped him. He drew back to find that tears trickled down her cheeks. He brushed them away with the tip of his finger, the fervency of their love and their breaths mingling, creating an intimate connection that went far beyond words.

As they sealed the promise of a lifetime, the world around them dissolved into an eternal moment. Their lasting embrace created an electrifying current that coursed through him, and his heart overflowed with awe.

When they finally pulled back, a lingering taste of her remained, a memory forever etched on his lips. He looked at Julia's beautiful face, where a glint of hope and love shimmered like stars on the water. "Let me ask you properly, please. Julia, will you marry me?"

What appeared to be bliss arose on her features, the sight almost tangible in the dim light. She nodded, her consent radiating through her countenance. "Thank you for that. I'd love to be your wife, to serve the Thousand Islanders with you here at Sister Island Lighthouse, and to share whatever adventures God may have in store for us—together—for the rest of our lives."

They both bubbled into laughter, a melodic song in the gentle rustle of the wind that whispered through the night, creating a refrain of delight that resonated with the very essence of their love.

His senses exploded in applause—the taste of kisses, the intensity in her touch, the scent of the river, the sight of her joy-filled countenance, and the sound of their laughter harmonizing with nature's evening melody. It was a symphony of love that transcended the boundaries of time and space in the very fabric of the lighthouse.

For a long while, they savored the moment in silence, but then they discussed their future. Excitement filled the air as they planned for a simple yet meaningful New Year's Eve wedding in the charming little town of Clayton.

By then, Granny's legal matters should be finalized, and Julia would be free to move on with life unencumbered. The quaint surroundings of Clayton, centrally located so Julia's relatives could come, would provide the perfect ambience for their union. They envisioned an intimate celebration surrounded by the support of friends and family to start the New Year right.

As night enveloped Sister Island in a quiet embrace, the stars above applauded their moment of profound connection and their hope for a blessed future.

Epilogue

The golden glow of the winter sun warmed the Clayton morning as Julia and William stood hand in hand at the entrance of the Hubbard House, a beautiful, three-story hotel, graced with wide porches on its main and upper floors. Fresh snow blanketed the streets, shimmering in the sun, creating a serene atmosphere for their New Year's Eve morning wedding. The historic hotel, adorned with abundant lights and winter-themed decorations, exuded an enchanting atmosphere for their special day.

"It's the perfect winter day, don't you think?" Julia's tummy tickled with anticipation. She wasn't nervous, really, just excited.

William planted a kiss on her cheek. "I can't wait to call you my wife and spend the rest of my life cherishing you."

She leaned into him, gratitude filling her heart as she wondered how life could be any sweeter than it was at this moment. But it would . . .

Hope-filled chatter filled the air as family and friends began to arrive to celebrate the union of two hearts. Small groups of well-wishers checked into the hotel, congregating in the wide hall to visit, or simply waiting for the festivities to start.

But then, Aunt Dee and Aunt Emma playfully tugged her away from William.

She blinked her surprise. "Where are we going, aunties? It's hours before the ceremony."

In the bustle of the hotel foyer, the aunts chuckled in unison, their eyes and their laughter filled with a conspiratorial delight.

"We need to prepare you for your nuptials, dear girl," Aunt Emma declared, her features flashing with mischief. "Bid your husband-to-be farewell, for our time with you starts now."

The excitement of the day tossed her emotions around like pebbles in the waves. She blew him a kiss. "I'll see you soon, sweetheart."

He blew her a kiss, too, and waved goodbye, a chuckle dancing on his words. "I can't wait, my lovely Gingersnap."

The trio of women navigated the narrow hallway to an elegantly furnished suite. Julia couldn't help but gasp at the opulence surrounding her. The room emanated a sense of cheerfulness and familiarity. "This reminds me so much of Granny's house."

Aunt Dee nodded knowingly. "Yes. That's why I chose it. Your granny is here with you, Julia. Your parents too." She touched her blouse over her heart. "There. They are celebrating with you."

A wave of melancholy washed over Julia, but she quickly pushed it away. Today was a day of joy, and nothing would dim the happiness she felt. "Thank you. It's a thoughtful choice of venue."

As she marveled at the surroundings, her cousin, Libby, emerged from around the corner, a mischievous grin on her face. "Hello, Julia. Congratulations on your nuptials."

Aunt Dee and Aunt Emma burst into laughter. "Surprise!"

Julia ran to Libby and enveloped her in a tight embrace. "I wasn't sure you'd come, being it's your honeymoon and all. Your wedding last week was marvelous, Libby. I hope mine will be too."

Libby squeezed her hands affectionately. "Thanks. Your wedding will be just as amazing, I'm sure. But your wedding night—and the days after—will surely be even better." Her cousin's eyes sparkled with secrets of intimacy, honeymoon happiness, and the marvels of newly married life. "Just you wait and see."

Julia pointed to Libby's necklace—three long strands of pearls. She touched her own single-strand heirloom. "We both have pearls. What else do we have in common?"

Libby giggled. "We'll have a lifetime to find out, won't we? But right now, I do have some-thing special to share with you." She hurried around the corner and held up the gown she had worn for her wedding. "I want you to wear this."

Julia gasped. "Really? Oh thank you, Libby."

Aunt Emma playfully *tsk*ed, interrupting the

moment between Julia and Libby. "All right, you two. Enough chatter. It's time to get the bride ready."

With gentle nudges, the aunts and Libby ushered Julia toward the private parlor, their joy palpable as they curled her hair and spritzed her with lemon verbena to prepare her for the most important day of her life. Nervous energy coursed through her veins, but the peace and comfort of the moment mingled to create a curious sort of ecstasy.

The room resounded with laughter and the rustling of fabrics as they helped Julia into the same breathtaking winter-white lace-trimmed gown Libby had worn just a week ago, which sparkled like freshly fallen snow.

Julia hugged her cousin again. "Thank you for letting me wear this. It's an extravagant gift, to be sure. Did Aunt Lucy come?"

"She couldn't. Sorry. But she sends her love." Libby held her at arm's length. "You look absolutely stunning, Julia. Even more beautiful than I did on my day."

Julia blushed, her hands flying to her cheeks to cool them. "Nonsense, but I never imagined wearing such a gorgeous dress. It's like a dream."

Aunt Emma chimed in. "The dress you had chosen to wear was nice, but your cousin Libby insisted on offering hers. She said sharing it could become a family tradition."

Libby nodded, a small sigh escaping her lips. "It's more than just a dress, Julia. It's a symbol of love and family. Wearing it will connect us through generations and create a bond that will go beyond words."

Julia's heart nearly burst with profound gratitude for her family—not only for the stunning gown but for the shared laughter, stories, and the sense of unity.

When all their ministrations were complete, Julia stood before the full-length mirror, her heart skipping a beat at the sight of herself. The gown, simple yet elegant, accentuated her features perfectly. Her aunts and cousin *ooh*ed and *ahh*ed over her radiant appearance, and silently, she agreed.

Aunt Dee touched her arm. "You're enchanting, my soon-to-be daughter."

Aunt Emma and Libby joined them, enveloping her in an affectionate group hug.

Libby, her eyes glistening with tears, whispered, "I'm so glad we're family!"

Julia blinked back tears of her own, overwhelmed by the love surrounding her. Just months ago, she was an orphan navigating a world of uncertainty. But now, not only did she have a loving husband awaiting her and a gracious mother-in-law supporting her, but she also had this wonderful extended family. The good Lord had orchestrated a future filled with hope, and Julia's heart brimmed with joy and gratitude.

Aunt Emma took her hand and chuckled. "It's time to get you hitched, niece."

The solemnity of the moment faded into light-hearted banter as they led Julia to the carriage that carried them to the church down the street, where she would become a lightkeeper's wife.

After they had shed their coats, Libby fluffed Julia's gown one last time before entering the sanctuary, arm in arm with Aunt Emma.

Aunt Dee kissed her on the cheek. "May I walk you down the aisle, daughter?"

She nodded, smiling from ear to ear. "I would love that, Aunt Dee. Thank you."

"It's Mother, if you please. No more 'Aunt Dee,' dearie."

Julia tipped her chin up as Mother opened the door to the sanctuary and the music began.

There William was, waiting for her at the altar. He chewed his lip and shifted his weight, his handsome face expressing both love and anticipation. She thanked God for this blessed day.

The ceremony unfolded with a melody of love, the music wafting through the church as they exchanged vows beneath flickering candles. The promise of forever resonated in their voices, filling the space with happiness.

As they sealed their vows with a kiss, the

audience erupted in cheerful applause. Arm in arm, they walked down the aisle, greeted by smiles and well-wishes from their loved ones.

The celebration continued back in the Hubbard House dining room, where the tantalizing aroma of a New Year's Eve wedding brunch filled the air. Tables adorned with winter floral arrangements, fine china, and costly silverware awaited them and their guests.

Amidst the delightful ambiance, Julia and her husband took their seats at the head table, exchanging glances that spoke volumes of love and joy and anticipation for the life ahead. When the meal was served, a blend of flavors mingled on her taste buds as she savored each bite. Laughter and heartfelt toasts filled the room.

After the brunch, William took her hand, leading her to a quiet corner adorned with mistletoe. Under its branches, he pulled her into a passionate kiss.

He whispered in her ear, his breath sending shivers down her spine. "This morning has been nothing short of magical. I couldn't have imagined a more perfect way to begin our journey together. And I can't wait to experience the rest of our lives together."

She smiled, her heart full. "William, you've made my dreams come true. I feel like the most blessed woman alive."

The hours passed in a blur of bounty, and as the

clock struck midnight, Julia and her new husband shared precious moments with family under a cascade of starlight.

The night concluded with a grand display of fireworks over the frozen river, illuminating the sky with bursts of color and shimmering reflections. Surrounded by the love of family and friends, they embraced the new year and the journey that awaited them as husband and wife.

Two days later, the quaint town of Clayton basked in the quiet charm of winter, snowflakes dancing in the crisp air as William stood with his bride in front of a lovely Victorian house.

Julia's brow furrowed. "Who lives here? Do you know them?"

He chuckled, excited to surprise her. "You'll see, sweetheart." He kissed her on the cheek before leading her up the steps to her new home.

With the money left over from Granny's inheritance, William had found the perfect place to call their winter home and pursue their shared passion for art. And though he hadn't yet seen the final results, Mother had organized family and friends to help her turn the house into a home while he and Julia enjoyed their honeymoon at the hotel.

Julia stopped on the porch. "It's a beautiful house. Does it belong to one of our wedding guests?"

He smirked, bursting with joy. He pressed his lips tight. The cheery Victorian stood proudly, a candle adorning each window and warm lamplight peeking through the glass.

She motioned toward the small sign by the door that read, *The Painters' Paradise*. "Is this an art gallery? I'd love to see other people's work."

He turned the knob, and the door creaked open, revealing the cheerful ambiance of their new abode. "It isn't an art gallery. Yet."

As they stepped inside, Julia's brow furrowed in confusion.

Mother sat by the fireplace knitting a pair of mittens, wearing a grin as wide as a crescent moon. "Welcome home, children! This is a gift from God and your granny, Julia. I hope you like it. William found it and wanted to surprise you."

Julia's mouth formed an O, and for several moments, she seemed to not comprehend his mother's announcement. But then, her eyes grew wide with understanding. "This is our home? Our winter home?" She searched his face for validation.

He grinned and kissed her soundly. "It is, my beautiful bride. It's our home—and our art studio."

Mother cackled loudly, obviously enjoying Julia's reaction. "It's so much nicer than the place we had rented in Chippewa Falls all those years, right, William?"

"Indeed. And you'll be able to visit with Libby and Emma, too, my sweet, spicy Gingersnap." His words resounded with affection and love. His Julia was truly a mixture of spirit and beauty.

Mother gestured to the room. "And look what Libby's and Emma's families did with the place. They've made this house into a home in but a few short days. Family sure is a blessing."

Julia laughed freely. "It sure is. I love what you all did. Thank you, Mother." She hurried over and hugged Mother soundly.

William led Julia into the front room. Natural light from the large windows overlooking a snow-covered street bathed the room in soft hues. Easels, canvases, and art supplies awaited their artistic touch. Julia's eyes sparkled with overflowing joy, and William couldn't hide his grin.

"This is perfect," Julia said on an exhale, taking it all in. "Our own space to paint and share our art with the community." She turned toward the piano in the corner of the room and gasped. "And a piano too?"

William nodded, his gaze wandering from the parlor-turned-art-studio to the blazing fireplace in the living room. "And imagine spending winter here, just a short distance from the Montonnas and Diepolders. It's like a dream come true, thanks to your granny, God rest her soul."

When she noticed the portrait of him above the

mantel, tears sprang to her eyes. "Oh, Mother! You put William's portrait there too? Thank you."

Mother beamed at them. "You captured him perfectly. Libby thought it'd be the perfect place for it, and she was right."

With a shared sense of hope, he and Julia explored every nook and cranny of their new winter home. Vintage furniture adorned the bedrooms, and the kitchen promised nights of shared meals and laughter.

As they peeked out the window at the backyard overlooking the frozen river, she turned to him and smiled. "I'll miss Sister Island for the winter, but I can't believe this is ours, my darling husband."

He wrapped his arms around her, the chill forgotten in the intensity of their love. "It's a new chapter in our lives, Julia. A home filled with love, creativity, and the promise of beautiful moments together."

They shared a kiss, grateful for the unexpected blessings that Granny's inheritance had brought and their family had prepared for them. Their winter home would not only be a sanctuary for their art but also a haven for their hearts.

Here, William and Julia embarked on the grandest adventure of all—the adventure of forever.

About the Author

Susan G Mathis is an international award-winning, multi-published author of stories set in the beautiful Thousand Islands, her childhood stomping ground in upstate New York. Susan has been published more than thirty times in full-length novels, novellas, and non-fiction books. She has thirteen in her fiction line, including *The Fabric of Hope: An Irish Family Legacy*, *Christmas Charity*, *Katelyn's Choice*, *Devyn's Dilemma*, *Sara's Surprise*, *Reagan's Reward*, *Colleen's Confession*, *Peyton's Promise*, *Rachel's Reunion*, *Mary's Moment*, *A Summer at Thousand Island House*, *Libby's Lighthouse* and *Julia's Joy*. Her book awards include three Illumination Book Awards, four American Fiction Awards, three Indie Excellence Book Awards, five Literary Titan Book Awards, a Golden Scroll Award, and a Selah Award.

Susan is also a published author of two premarital books, two children's picture books, stories in a dozen compilations, and hundreds of published articles. Susan makes her home in Colorado Springs and enjoys traveling around the world but returns each summer to enjoy the Thousand Islands. Visit www.SusanGMathis.com/fiction for more

Acknowledgments

To Judy Keeler, my wonderful historical editor, who combs through my manuscripts for accuracy. Because of her, you can trust that my stories are historically correct. And to Mary Alice Snetsinger, who made sure the lighthouse information was accurate.

To my wonderful Beta Team, Judy, Laurie, Donna, Barb, Melinda, and Davalynn, who inspire me with your kindness, faithfulness, and wisdom. Thanks for all your hard work and wise input.

To my amazing publisher, Misty Beller, and rock-star editor, Denise Weimer. Thanks to you, I'm soaring on the wings of my writing journey.

And to all my dear friends who have journeyed with me in my writing. Thanks for your emails, social media posts, and especially for your reviews. Most of all, thanks for your friendship.

And to God, from whom all good gifts come. Without You, there would never be a dream or the ability to fulfill that dream. Thank you!

Author's Note

I hope you enjoyed *Julia's Joy*. If you've read any of my other books, you know that I love introducing history to my readers through fictional stories. I hope this story sparks interest in our amazing past, especially the fascinating past of the marvelous Thousand Islands.

Sister Island Lighthouse and the Dodge family are real, though Julia is fashioned in my imagination. William took over as lightkeeper when his father died in 1893, but William didn't have pleurisy. And don't you just love Mrs. Dodge, whom you met in both *A Summer at Thousand Island House* and *Libby's Lighthouse*? I sure do. Also note that some of the timing is a little different than the historic record as I took a bit of creative license in bringing this story to life.

This is the second of three lighthouse novels, and I hope you'll enjoy them all. In the series, you'll meet the Row family women—Libby, Julia, and Emma—as they navigate the isolation, danger, and hope for lasting love at three different St. Lawrence River lighthouses. In book one, *Libby's Lighthouse*, you'll experience life at Tibbetts Point Lighthouse, and in book three, *Emma's Engagement*, you'll enjoy the famous Rock Island Lighthouse.

Center Point Large Print
600 Brooks Road / PO Box 1
Thorndike, ME 04986-0001 USA

(207) 568-3717

US & Canada:
1 800 929-9108
www.centerpointlargeprint.com